Para mi madre y mi padre

Brava

A Latina Lawyer's
Path to Empowerment

Adriana Palomares

BALBOA.PRESS
A DIVISION OF HAY HOUSE

Balboa Press books may be ordered through booksellers or by contacting:

Balboa Press
A Division of Hay House
1663 Liberty Drive
Bloomington, IN 47403
www.balboapress.com
844-682-1282

Because of the dynamic nature of the Internet, any web addresses or links contained in this book may have changed since publication and may no longer be valid. The views expressed in this work are solely those of the author and do not necessarily reflect the views of the publisher, and the publisher hereby disclaims any responsibility for them.

The author of this book does not dispense medical advice or prescribe the use of any technique as a form of treatment for physical, emotional, or medical problems without the advice of a physician, either directly or indirectly. The intent of the author is only to offer information of a general nature to help you in your quest for emotional and spiritual well-being. In the event you use any of the information in this book for yourself, which is your constitutional right, the author and the publisher assume no responsibility for your actions.

Illustration by: Soni Lopez-Chavez

Print information available on the last page.

ISBN: 979-8-7652-4593-4 (sc)
ISBN: 979-8-7652-4595-8 (hc)
ISBN: 979-8-7652-4594-1 (e)

Library of Congress Control Number: 2023918960

Balboa Press rev. date: 10/11/2023

CONTENTS

CHAPTER 1

Ojos Negros

"PLEASE DON'T COME ANY CLOSER. I'LL DO AS YOU SAY," JUANA pleaded, her slim, fifteen-year-old body trembling. The sound of horse hooves grew louder, causing her soul to yearn for escape. Kneeling on the river bank, clutching a pair of wet linen trousers, she dreaded the moment she would have to face him. For two years, she had managed to elude him, but now the inevitable had arrived. The urge to throw herself into the river and let the current swallow her whole overwhelmed her. Squeezing the wet trousers tighter, she felt utterly powerless. Slowly, she rose to her feet, and a mixture of water and urine trickled down her legs, drenching her already wet skirt. With great hesitation, she turned to confront him, the trousers slipping from her hand. Her instinct was to keep her gaze fixed on the ground, but eventually, she looked up, surveying her surroundings. Her hope was to see other women washing clothes by the river. If at least one were present, she could run to her, seeking protection from this man in their shared company. However, she found herself utterly alone. Knowing there was nowhere to escape, she lifted her eyes to meet his, despair evident in her black orbs, reminiscent of a fawn about to be hunted by a wolf. Lucho had appeared suddenly from behind a grove of willow trees, patiently lying in wait for this moment. The lush trees seemed to create a barrier, enclosing them in a space from which she could find no escape. The rushing sound of the river masked her rapid, uncontrollable heartbeat, which threatened to give way to a panic attack.

"I will marry you, Lucho, but please don't hurt me," she stammered, her voice trembling. He took a step closer, poised to pounce. In her panic, she instinctively stepped back, nearly stumbling into the river. The terror in her eyes caught his attention, halting him in his tracks. Placing his hands on his waist, he looked away, suppressing his primal desire. Taking a deep breath, he spoke, his voice laced with forced composure.

"I'm glad to hear that you wish to marry me, Juana. I will arrange a meeting with your parents in the coming days." He tilted his straw sombrero slightly and took a few steps back. Mounting his horse, he rode off, knowing that their wedding would take place in a few weeks. This encounter marked the first and only interaction between my grandmother, Juana, and my grandfather, Luis Granados, before they were wed.

My maternal grandmother, affectionately known as Mamá Juanita, was only thirteen years old when she first noticed Lucho's unwavering gaze upon her. She was on her way to collect dough from the mill when he rode past on his horse, fixating his eyes on her. The intensity of his stare unsettled her. His twenty-three-year-old frame, mounted on the horse, exuded a commanding presence. Trying to shake off the unease, she quickened her pace and turned the corner, avoiding any further eye contact. From the moment she began menstruating, her mother had warned her against making eye contact with men. She had been instructed to avoid isolated encounters with men at all costs, as such encounters could lead to forced marriages and bring disgrace upon her family. At the age of thirteen, she didn't fully comprehend the implications of marriage, but she understood the concept of disgrace through her parents' tumultuous relationship. Having witnessed her father's violent tendencies and his anger-fueled outbursts, particularly when he drank *aguardiente*, she concluded that all men were like him: rough, callous, and prone to anger.

Thus, a sense of terror consumed her whenever she thought about her mother's warning. Each time she passed men on the streets, she averted her gaze, keeping her eyes fixed on the ground.

When my grandmother first shared this story with me, I couldn't help but ask her why she agreed to marry Lucho. It hadn't occurred to me that she had no choice in the matter. In those days, courtship didn't exist. Women lacked the agency to choose their own husbands. Refusing to marry Lucho would have resulted in him forcibly taking her and violating her by the riverbank. Subsequently, he would have taken her to his parents' home, announcing to her family that she had been "*robada*"— stolen. Being robada was the dishonorable way of getting married. Women who were robadas brought shame and disgrace upon their families. Therefore, accepting the marriage proposal without resistance was considered the moral path into wedded life. Agreeing to marry him would grant her the honor of marrying "*de blanco*," a symbol of purity. While my grandfather turned out to be less of a monster than Mamá Juanita had expected, the way he had coerced her into the marriage still troubled me. Yet, as she would say, "That's just how things were back then. Women didn't have a say."

Mamá Juanita, the daughter of a farmer and a *curandera*, was born on a moonlit night. Her tan skin resembled the clay found along the riverbank. With abundant straight black hair and big, dark eyes, she possessed a striking appearance. However, her early years were anything but easy. She was an only child, as my great-grandmother had various miscarriages. She was unable to bear more children after my great-grandfather stabbed her womb with a sickle, nearly taking her life. Mamá Juanita, a mere five-year-old at the time, had witnessed the horrifying incident, which had silenced her. It wasn't until she had her first child that her voice returned, though she remained largely reticent. This tragic event was something I had never discussed with Mamá Juanita. My mother had warned me that it was a painful memory for her and should be kept as one of the family's "secrets," joining the ranks of many other undisclosed stories. It was difficult for me to imagine a life without hearing Mamá Juanita's voice, and perhaps that's why I cherished every opportunity to listen to her speak. Her voice was gentle, carrying a wealth of wisdom within it. After my great-grandfather's attack on my great-grandmother, Mamá Juanita had to grow up quickly. Her mother was unable to walk for months. My great-grandfather fled the town and remained in hiding for several years until the situation settled and he could return as if nothing had happened. He never faced justice for his actions. Thus, at the tender age of five, Mamá Juanita had to learn how to make tortillas, sew, wash clothes by the river, light fires in the makeshift stove, and prepare the herbal remedies, poultices, and ointments that my great-grandmother used in her healing sessions and sold for a living. My great-grandmother never fully recovered, relying on Mamá Juanita for assistance with daily tasks and chores. She took her deep into the caves within the nearby volcanoes, where medicinal mushrooms and herbs grew in abundance. Inside the semi-darkness of the caves, with only faint rays of sunlight filtering through the crevices, Mamá Juanita's black eyes became her guiding light. She collected the herbs in an old, straw basket while my great-grandmother offered instructions. It was no surprise that Mamá Juanita became a skilled herbalist, mastering the art of *curanderismo*. She hoped that being the daughter of a curandera would spare her from a forced marriage. The predominantly Catholic townsfolk frowned upon curanderismo, considering it a form of witchcraft. Her mother-in-law, Doña Rosario, vehemently opposed her son's marriage to the daughter of a curandera. Doña Rosario, a devout Catholic, believed that such practices were *cosas del diablo*— associated with witchcraft. However, Mamá Juanita's heritage failed to protect her from her destined fate.

According to my mother, Mamá Juanita's life as a married woman was arduous. Doña Rosario treated her as a servant, ridiculing her for her silence and referring to her as *la bruja muda*—the mute witch. Once married to Papá Lucho, Mamá Juanita never created another poultice or ointment. Doña Rosario imposed Catholicism upon her, compelling her to abandon all teachings passed down by her mother. Mamá Juanita gradually transformed into a devoutly religious woman who raised her children to fear God. According to my mother, she was a strict mother, indoctrinating her children into Catholicism and ensuring their attendance at Sunday Mass. She instilled a fear of God in them, using it as a means of maintaining their good behavior. As a grandmother, however, she was loving and indulgent. Kind, patient, and nurturing, she exuded an angelic essence that intrigued me.

During my childhood, my bond with Mamá Juanita was extraordinary. I was profoundly drawn to her energy, much like a hummingbird to honeysuckle. I loved visiting her rustic cottage, which boasted a beautiful garden at its center. An orange tree stood proudly amid lemon, guava, and papaya trees. I spent hours in her garden, cutting flowers from her potted plants and adorning my hair with them. In my imagination, I transformed into a bride on her wedding day, wearing a magnificent flower crown, a long white dress, and a sparkling veil. I twirled around the garden, envisioning myself waltzing with my father. At times, my attention would shift to the butterflies and dragonflies fluttering through the garden, and I would chase after them. From a distance, Mamá Juanita observed me, eventually calling me to her side. I would settle onto her lap, enveloped in her embrace, as she cradled me and hummed "Amor Eterno." As I lay my head on her shoulder, she whispered in my ear, "Lucia, tú naciste para cambiar nuestro linaje. Tú eres la luz de nuestro destino. Tu espíritu es como la lava que flota lenta, pero poderosa desde las entrañas de los volcanes." ["Lucia, you were born to change our lineage. You are the light of our destiny. Your spirit is like the lava that flows slowly, yet powerfully, from the depths of the volcanoes."] Perplexed, I would look at her and inquire about the meaning of her words.

"How could I fulfill that destiny?" I asked.

Her response never wavered. "Solo ponte en las manos de Dios." ["Just put yourself in God's hands."] Her endearing smile and softened black eyes conveyed more than words ever could. It wasn't until many years later, in the darkest moment of my life, that I finally understood the depth of Mamá Juanita's message.

CHAPTER 2

El Romance

My name is Lucia Inocencio Granados. I was born in El Romance, Guanajuato, México, a quaint colonial town nestled among seven volcanoes. My town was known for its fertile lands, which produced giant crops such as tomatoes, cabbage, and carrots. The town was abundant with avocado, eucalyptus, and olive trees. Sunflowers, *cempasuchil*, and lavender propagated through the hillsides; wild agave salmiana grew within the canyons of the volcanoes. At nighttime, millions of stars adorned the sky. The Inocencio and Granados families had settled there many years before. Both families were descendants of farmers who took care of the land, and in return, the land took care of them for generations. However, this way of making a living became unsustainable. In the 1970s, rural unemployment forced many Mexican men, including my father and uncles, to cross into the United States in search of work that would help them survive and support their families in México. As a migrant worker, my father was absent for prolonged periods during my early childhood. He earned better wages in the US and returned to México periodically to reconnect with his family.

Our house was situated on a piece of land at the foot of one of the volcanoes. My father inherited the plot of land from his father, Papá Merced. He divided his land into smaller lots and gave one to each of his children. This meant that all my paternal aunts, uncles, and cousins lived nearby. Even though we had our own houses, we shared a large dirt courtyard. Right in the middle of that courtyard stood a magnificent guava tree, providing us with juicy, sweet, pink guavas and offering refreshing shade on scorching summer days. That courtyard became our playground and our gathering place on lazy Sunday afternoons.

I spent the first eight years of my life in El Romance, enveloped between the magical beauty of my town, the bliss of childhood, and the despair caused by the constant absence of my father. Every time my father and my uncles migrated to El Norte, Papá Merced, became our guardian. He promised his sons that he would watch over their children while they were gone. Twice a month, he took my cousins and me to the top of the volcano closest to our house. We hiked on a dirt road that had been made by grazing cattle, with my grandfather's donkey, Ignacia, graciously carrying all the essentials for our picnic: a *petate* to sit on, a *comal* to warm tortillas, a large *guaje* filled with fresh water, corn from Papá Merced's *milpa*, fresh beans, and tortillas that my *abuela* packed for us. We sat near a creek, under a huge, leafy avocado tree. Papá Merced made a swing out of a piece of wood and rope, and we took turns swinging while he roasted corn over a makeshift fire pit. My older cousins swam in the creek and held swimming competitions while the rest of us watched and waited for our turn on the swing. I loved my grandfather, and I loved going on adventures with him, but I often wished it was my own father who took me on these bonding experiences. I struggled to understand why my father had to be away, even as my childhood days were filled with precious memories.

***

Leticia's birth was one of the most invigorating experiences of my childhood. At the age of four, I witnessed her birth. In El Romance, women gave birth at home with the assistance of midwives and older female relatives. I had been sick with a stubborn asthma flare-up in the days prior to my mother going into labor. I did not want to let go of my mother's arms. It was as if I sensed that some magnificent event was about to occur, and I wanted to be near her to experience it. I still remember clinging to my mother's bosom tightly. However, when contractions overpowered her, she threw me into Mamá Juanita's arms. Mamá Juanita took me into her arms, and I witnessed my mother wail in excruciating pain. As the contractions grew stronger and Leticia was closer to entering the world, my young brain aimed to untangle what was happening. When the midwife walked in the room, she looked elfish in the dim light, illuminated only by various oil lanterns and thick white candles. She was an older woman with white braided hair, and a black *rebozo* covered her head as she appeared calm and determined. Suddenly, my mother shrieked even louder, and the midwife hastily removed her rebozo. Mamá Juanita handed me over to my paternal grandmother, Mamá Cuca, and hurried to my mother's bedside. She wiped the sweat from my mother's forehead with a white rag and held her hand tightly. Mamá Cuca began to pray, while a young woman I didn't recognize handed the midwife a sharp-looking object. Kneeling between my mother's widely spread legs, the midwife looked focused while Mamá Cuca fired words of encouragement.

"Push Ana! Push harder! Push! It's coming! It's coming!"

Enticed and focused solely on the space between my mother's legs, I saw blood trickle. Suddenly, something emerged, and I watched in stillness. Within seconds, Leticia came into the world, crying louder than my mother had been. "It's a girl! It's a girl!" exclaimed the midwife. Leticia looked like a tiny creature, her black hair smeared with blood across her fragile forehead. Her body was minuscule. The midwife wrapped her in white cloth and placed her on my mother's chest. As Leticia landed there, she stopped crying and began sucking her hand. My mother's screams had transformed into joyful sobs. With a devoted gaze, she explored every inch of Leticia. "Look, Lucia, it's your little sister," Mamá Cuca said. Remaining perplexed in Mamá Cuca's arms, I felt a profound change within me. A warm sensation grew in my heart, unblocking my lungs, normalizing my breathing, and dissipating my asthma. A very special feeling began to flourish. Leticia's birth became my earliest and most vivid childhood memory.

After Leticia's birth, despite my tender age, I took it upon myself to assist my mother in watching her, changing her diapers, and feeding her. I also began to help my mother with chores. I remembered how much pain my mother had been through, and I felt compelled to help. My favorite part was washing Leticia's tiny clothes on the cement washboard. It felt like I was washing my doll's dresses. I grabbed a small wooden stool and placed it in front of the washboard. I stood on top of it and spread the garments on the washboard as I had seen my mother do. With my right hand, I grabbed a small, red, plastic pail and leaned into the cement water tank to fetch water. I soaked the clothes, mimicking my mother's actions. With both hands, I grabbed a big, pink bar of soap and rubbed it on the clothes. I squeezed the soapy water out, one garment at a time. My mother watched me from a distance, making sure the stool did not tilt and cause me to fall into the water tank.

As the years passed, my mother urged me to always behave well because Leticia was watching. What example would I set for her? When I threw a tantrum because I wanted my mother to buy me candy at the Mercado, and she refused, she reminded me of Leticia's observant eyes, prompting me to stop crying because I wouldn't want her to mimic the same behavior. When she dropped me off at kindergarten, she emphasized the importance of good behavior and striving for good grades so that I could assist Leticia with her homework when she went to school. When I became a teenager and had a fit because my mother wouldn't let me spend the night at a friend's house, I was admonished for setting a bad example for Leticia. My life and Leticia's became intertwined. I was pressured to be the best role model for her, and she was pressured to reach the high bar I had been forced to set. I became an overachiever in school and everything extracurricular I did. I developed a competitive nature and strived to be the best student in my classroom. Leticia and I were constantly compared, we had to live and grow under each other's shadow. "Lucia has the brains, but Leticia has the beauty," I would often hear Mamá Cuca say.

Leticia grew into a beautiful little girl, with long, straight hair that curled at the ends, in a light brown shade. Her honey-colored eyes and chubby, rosy cheeks added to her charm. She closely resembled Mamá Cuca, who was tall, slender, had light skin, and green eyes. Mamá Cuca had traces of gold in her white hair and often proudly claimed her Spanish ancestry. However, despite Mamá Cuca's good looks, her beauty was overshadowed by her harshness. She possessed a strong will and imposed strict rules. She was brutally honest, short-tempered, and unhesitant to swear in front of her grandchildren. "Hijos de su chingada Madre!" I would hear her swear when she was upset at any particular grandchild, except her favorite grandchildren. She was the kind of grandmother who openly showed favoritism toward certain grandchildren, and Leticia was one of her favorites. On weekends, she would gather her favored grandchildren, prepare hot chocolate for them, and offer each a piece of *pan dulce*. The non-favored grandchildren, including myself, would simply look and try to understand why we didn't get a piece of bread.

"They are smaller than you," she said to justify herself. So, Leticia found comfort and love in Mamá Cuca's presence, and although it made me feel jealous, I sought solace in the connection I shared with Mamá Juanita.

I, on the other hand, had a darker complexion and black eyes, resembling my mother and Mamá Juanita. Furthermore, I developed a peculiar illness that caused my skin to break out in a rash. My mother and I endured countless sleepless nights as I faced asthma attacks that drained the oxygen from my body, leaving me dehydrated, exhausted, and weak for several days. On other nights, an uncontrollable itch would torment my skin, causing immense discomfort. As I cried, my mother held my small hands tightly, but when she succumbed to exhaustion, I would scratch my scabbed skin until it bled. There were nights when I woke up with my head resting on her lap, seeking relief. Sometimes, I would awaken her, begging her to tie my hands to prevent scratching. My physical condition made me a target for bullying. I had to learn to ignore the frequent comments and intrusive questions posed by both classmates and strangers. "What's wrong with her?" "Why is her skin like that?" "Have you taken her to the doctor?" These questions, among many others, bombarded my mother every time we ventured out in public. Little did people know that my mother longed to understand why I had developed this illness. She had taken me to countless doctors, including a curandera, and no medicine or poultice cured my condition. For years, we faced scrutiny when we ourselves lacked answers to my condition. Gradually, I became ashamed of my appearance and began to despise how I looked.

I often wondered whether my dreadful skin was the reason why I was not one of Mamá Cuca's favorites. She would often remark, with a tone of repugnance, that I resembled Mamá Juanita. "You're dark like your grandmother Juana," she would say. Though I couldn't comprehend her reasoning, her body language and tone felt like a sharp knife piercing my young heart. Fortunately, my cleverness earned me some favor in her eyes. I was one of the few grandchildren whom Mamá Cuca trusted to run errands. In her opinion, I spoke like a grown woman, and despite my young voice, the messages I conveyed were clear.

Despite Mamá Cuca's hurtful behavior, I was always obedient when she called upon me for help. "Lucia! Come here, child!" she would yell. Whether it was to deliver a message to a neighbor or another adult, or to fetch tortillas from the nearby tortilleria, I was always ready to assist. I relished the task of picking up tortillas because only the older granddaughters were entrusted with this responsibility. I had proven myself responsible enough to handle such errands. I knew how to count money and made sure I received the correct change. I went the extra mile to please and impress her. However, no matter how much I tried, I never received a compliment from her. Mamá Cuca particularly disliked when I offered my unsolicited opinions during adult conversations or asked too many questions. While others found my wit fascinating, Mamá Cuca appeared annoyed. She would tell my mother that I was being *metiche*—meddlesome—often leading to trouble for me. I frequently overheard her saying to my mother, "Be careful with this one, Ana. Esta te salió bien brava [defying]. It's as if she has fire in her blood. She'll give you many headaches. You should be stricter with her."

My mother urged me to be quiet, especially when I was around Mamá Cuca. When I asked why I couldn't speak my mind, she simply said, "You know how your grandmother is. Let's avoid problems with her. Now hurry up and stop asking questions, *niña*." I wanted to know more, but I had learned not to question my elders. I understood that when I was told "no," it meant no explanation followed, even though my curious mind yearned to make sense of things. I struggled to comprehend my grandmother's remarks and my mother's explanations, and I began associating chattiness and curiosity with negative characteristics. It seemed to me that being submissive and quiet was praised, while being independent and expressive was seen as rebellious. I absorbed it all in my subconscious mind and sought solace by climbing up our guava tree, where I would spend long periods of time. I would lie flat on my back on one of the thicker branches, gazing up at the sky, daydreaming about my father's return. Though I barely knew him, I missed the idea of him, and his absence often robbed me of the joyfulness of childhood.

One summer afternoon, a few weeks before my eighth birthday, I returned home from school proudly wearing a gold star on my forehead, indicating that I had earned the best grade in class. I longed for Mamá Cuca to notice it and compliment me. I searched for her and stood before her with a smile. She looked at me, scanning me from head to toe, noticing the star. Instead of praising me, she pretended not to see it. "Niña, estoy ocupada, ¿no miras?" ["Girl, I am busy, can't you see?"], she said coldly, dismissing me from her kitchen. Her indifference shattered my heart. I lowered my head and shrugged my shoulders in disappointment. With all my heart, I wished for my father to be there and comfort me. As I walked back through the courtyard that led to my house, my broken heart was interrupted by commotion. Several of my older cousins ran past me, heading toward the street, with our dog Benito barking behind them. My mother emerged from the kitchen, looking delighted, and hurriedly followed them.

"¡Ya llegó mi tío Poncho del Norte!" ¡Ya llegó mi tío Poncho del Norte! ¡Lucia, llegó tu papá!" ["Uncle Poncho has arrived from the North! Uncle Poncho has arrived from the North! Lucia, your father has arrived!"]. Their exhilarated screams echoed in my head for a few moments, and I felt as if I were in a daze. I ran toward the street too. As I reached the door, I stood in disbelief, gasping and covering my mouth with my small hand. Within a quarter of a mile from me stood the vibrant, loving man who gave me life. I could barely recognize him, yet his brown face illuminated with a joyful smile reminded me that he was my father. He carried a massive black sack over his shoulder, which didn't seem to burden his steady pace. My cousins leaped onto him, embracing him tightly. Benito sniffed him all over while wagging his tail. The sound of my father's laughter mingled with my cousins' giggles, filling our cobblestone street. I stood frozen, absorbing the moment, as my eyes grew moist. My father had returned from El Norte.

CHAPTER 3

Bracero

My father, Alfonso Ruben Inocencio, or "Poncho" as he was known in our town, first migrated to the United States in 1962 at the age of eighteen. He learned about the *Bracero* program and decided to sign up for it. The Bracero program was a bilateral agreement between the Mexican and United States governments that allowed Mexican men to legally migrate to the United States for short-term agricultural labor contracts. From 1942 to 1964, over four million contracts were signed, with many braceros returning multiple times on different contracts. Knowing there was a quota system in place and that the admissions process was competitive, my father embarked on the journey north, hoping to obtain a US work permit. He traveled with his childhood friend, Ruben, from El Romance to Empalme, Sonora, where the Mexican government had offices to process applications for potential bracero workers. They arrived at the government offices at dawn, aware that they would have to endure long hours of waiting to register. With empty stomachs, having only coffee and *bolillo*, my father and Ruben persevered through the tedious wait. My father told me that the line of men waiting to register stretched for several blocks. Once registered, they underwent a physical examination, which according to my father, required them to strip naked in public to be checked for venereal disease and hemorrhoids, and to be "disinfected" by being sprayed with a pesticide. They underwent X-rays and a blood test. Those who passed the exam received a temporary permit. Unfortunately, Ruben, who had lung issues, was deemed unfit for the program and had to return to El Romance.

My father was granted a permit and the following morning, he walked to the train station to begin his journey into the US. He presented his permit and received a lunch bag containing a cold sandwich, an apple, and a hard oatmeal cookie. He was transported to Mexicali and from there to the Calexico port of entry. Thereafter, he, along with many other Braceros, boarded a bus headed to San Jose, California, where he began his first contract, picking tomatoes in the fields of a major US produce grower's farm.

The days as a bracero were extraordinarily challenging for my father. The working conditions were inhumane, with inadequate housing, food, and healthcare provided. The hours were long, and the labor was physically demanding. The workers slept in overcrowded bunk beds in barracks that turned into ovens during the summer months. The blaring communal alarm that rang at six o'clock in the morning for breakfast was a sound my father could never get used to. Breakfast was served in a large warehouse-like building with poor lighting. Breakfast consisted of eggs, toast, beans, oatmeal, and black coffee.

After breakfast, my father and the other workers in his group boarded a bus that took them directly to the farm. He would begin working as soon as the sun rose and would end his shift at sunset. Throughout the day, he spent countless hours bending at the waist, picking tomatoes and filling boxes with them. The workers were paid based on the number of tomato boxes they filled. The more boxes they filled, the more money they earned. My father shared stories of how some mischievous workers would steal tomatoes from younger workers in order to fill more boxes for themselves. Arguments frequently erupted among the workers, who were stressed, underfed, and lacking proper rest. They were treated as commodities and exploited to meet the demands of large US agricultural companies, serving the interests of both the US and Mexican governments. After the Bracero program ended in 1964, my father and all braceros were deported from the United States. Finding himself without a plan, my father took a bus back to El Romance.

He returned to working as a farmer alongside Papá Merced, planting and harvesting corn and alfalfa. He spent his days toiling in the fields, plowing the volcanic ground beneath his feet, receiving meager compensation for his labor. However, his mind was consumed by a different passion: music. My father had developed a deep love for music from a very young age. He dreamed of becoming a musician but had never had the courage to share his dream with anyone. When he finally gathered the courage to share his dream with Papá Merced, his father responded with dismay, asserting that dreams were only for those with money. "La gente como nosotros nació para trabajar, no para esas pendejadas." ["People like us were born to work, not for nonsense"], my abuelo had told him. In a patriarchal society where men were expected to work the land and provide for their families until their dying days, Papá Merced couldn't fathom his son pursuing a different path. Undeterred by his father's disapproval, my father sought support from Mamá Cuca. As the family matriarch, Mamá Cuca, possessed a certain level of autonomy within societal norms and she was determined to help her son achieve his dream. She enlisted the help of their neighbor, Mento, a blind man abandoned by his parents as a child but skilled in playing the guitar. Mamá Cuca convinced Mento to teach my father how to play the guitar in exchange for a warm daily meal. Eager to embark on his musical journey, my father wasted no time in starting his guitar lessons. With Mento's guidance, he quickly became proficient in playing *ranchero* tunes. The arrangement proved beneficial for both of them. Mento, who had rarely experienced a sense of accomplishment in his fifty years of life, found fulfillment in helping my father cultivate his talent. Meanwhile, my father began to believe that his dream of becoming a musician was within reach. On his twenty-first birthday, Mamá Cuca surprised my father with a remarkable gift: a guitar, which she had purchased with her savings of fifty pesos from a man at the flea market. This precious gift marked the beginning of my father's life as a musician. Together with some friends, he formed a mariachi band and traveled to México City, where they played at Plaza Garibaldi for tips.

As years passed, my father envisioned himself returning to the US and performing in bars frequented by Mexican migrant workers, where they sought solace from their nostalgia and unfulfilled lives through heartfelt *corrido* songs. Besides, playing music and earning dollars was a double win for him. Convincing some of his bandmates to join him, my father saved every peso possible until he had enough to make the journey north. He and three of his bandmates set off to pursue his dream in the United States. While attempting to cross the border illegally, they met a smuggler who promised to help them cross easily. This was the first time they attempted to cross illegally and thus were naïve about the process. They trusted the smuggler, who turned out to be a conman. He led them through the Sonoran Desert on a perilous journey and abandoned them in the darkness of the desert after stripping them of their money. Lost, tired, and helpless, they sought refuge under a pile of rocks. The following day, they embarked on a grueling walk that almost cost them their lives. Fortunately, a good Samaritan found them and took them to a migrant refuge in Piedras Negras, where they recovered from dehydration. Two of my father's bandmates decided to return to El Romance, realizing the hardships were too great. However, my father and his friend Chava remained in Piedras Negras, doing odd jobs and performing for tips at the main plaza.

When they saved enough money, they hired another *coyote* and made a successful second attempt at crossing the border into Texas. A truck driver who found them on the side of the highway agreed to drive them to Chicago. In Chicago, they initially slept on the streets until finding shelter in a church. With the help of the priest, they secured jobs and rented a small shared room. My father worked long hours in a milk factory during the day and played with Chava at bars during the night. The wages he earned in the United States far surpassed what he could have earned in México in a year. Realizing the financial opportunities in the United States, my father stayed in Chicago for three years, working hard and saving money. He sent some money back to his parents in El Romance and saved the rest to purchase musical instruments to fulfill his dream of starting a band.

Unfortunately, at the end of his third year in Chicago, Mamá Cuca fell ill and my father returned to El Romance before being able to accomplish his dream. He used most of his savings to pay for Mamá Cuca's medical treatment. Guilt-ridden, my father decided to stay and try his luck in El Romance. Though unable to buy all the instruments he had hoped for, he acquired a big speaker, amplifier, and a new guitar with the remaining funds. Within weeks, he recruited local musicians who already owned their own instruments, and they formed a *norteño* band called Los Luceros del Romance. For several years, they played at festivals, weddings, *quinceañeras*, and other events in the *pueblo* and neighboring cities, enjoying a successful run. However, misfortune struck when one unfortunate morning on their way back home, their van was intercepted by armed individuals. The thieves stole their van, along with all their instruments and profits from the gig. Faced with this setback, my father had to make a difficult decision. He had already married my mother, and my brother Pedro was on the way. With no other recourse, he turned to migrating to the United States for work. During the summers, my father worked in the fields of central California, while in the winters, he played guitar for a norteño band at a bar in Los Angeles. He continued this pattern of migrating between México and the United States for many years, seeking employment and supporting his growing family.

Meanwhile, my mother used the money that he sent to start building our house in El Romance. I can still remember her saying, "Your father sacrifices so much to build this house. When it's complete, the sacrifice will have been worth it." However, I couldn't help but feel a trivial resentment toward it. I blamed it for keeping my father away. Years later, when I returned to El Romance, I saw our house with different eyes. The house remained unfinished. It appeared desolate, empty, and neglected; time had taken its toll and was on the verge of reducing it to ruins. Our house was supposed to be a two-story building, but from the outside, it resembled a cement bunker. On the ground level, there were three semi-complete bedrooms, while the second floor remained unfinished. Instead of tiled floors, we had a cold, bare cement surface that had felt harsh on our feet. The walls, made of red brick, were incomplete, leaving visible crevices where scorpions found refuge. As a child, my mother taught me to shake my shoes before wearing them to ensure that no venomous creature had crawled inside and might sting me. The black metal windows and doors were still standing, but some of the glass was missing. Despite its unpolished appearance, those windows and doors had once provided us shelter during cold winter months and mosquito-filled summers. The long hallway was the only part of the house with finished, smooth walls. My mother had painted them pastel green, giving them a weathered look. I could almost hear the echoes of Pedro's and Leticia's laughter echoing through the hall. The hallway led directly to the courtyard.

The kitchen was meant to be adjacent to the courtyard, but all that remained was a skeletal red brick structure without walls. On the ceiling, a large soot spot marked the place where my mother's *manteca*-based cooking had left its trace. I could still see the markings on the cement floor where the propane stove and our old refrigerator had stood. A green, rusted cabinet that stored our blue pewter dinnerware had stood across. Our cookware had hung from nails on the brick wall, and in the center of it all, our wooden dining table, with its four flamboyantly painted green chairs, had stood firmly. Next to the makeshift kitchen was the bathroom, a small and dark four-wall cement room with a flowery cloth curtain serving as its door. I remember how the lack of running water made showering a long and tedious process. My mother had to fetch water from a tank in the patio and heat it up on the stove. She would then carry the pail of hot water into the bathroom, mixing it with cooler water in a larger metal tub to make it warm. We called it "showering *a jicaradas*," which involved scooping water from the tub using a small plastic pail and pouring it over ourselves to lather and rinse off the soap. I disliked showering on winter days because the cold air would seep in through the cloth curtain, stinging my body while I tried to wash away the soap.

It struck me that many houses in El Romance remained incomplete, and I had always wondered why so many of them had unfinished second stories. It wasn't until I returned that I made sense of it all. The US immigration crackdown in the mid-1980s disrupted the once easy and constant flow of border crossings, forcing many undocumented migrants to permanently stay north of the border, fearing they wouldn't be able to return to work. Typically, the men would migrate first, finding work in El Norte and sending money back to their wives in their hometowns. The wives would oversee the construction of the first story, yet as construction of the second story took place, the wives and children would join the men in the United States. Once they left, many families didn't return for years, if ever. Their lives were uprooted and replanted in different cities across the United States, like fertile seeds finding new ground. The unfinished second stories of countless houses in El Romance became silent testaments to the stories of migrant families, including my own.

CHAPTER 4

Ana Granados

ANA GRANADOS WAS BORN IN THE NORTHERN SIDE OF EL ROMANCE near the river and the olive tree orchards. Slim and with dark brown hair, she inherited Mamá Juanita's black eyes. Ana loved running barefoot on the dirt furrows that wound through the green fields and tall maize crops. She possessed remarkable speed and agility. Even at the age of fifteen, she retained the spirit of a young girl, playing games like hide-and-seek and *la rueda de San Miguel* with her younger siblings and other children from the town. She was the second child, but the first girl born to Mamá Juanita and Papá Lucho. Ana Granados was my mother. Mamá Juanita, recognizing the limitations and challenges she faced in her own life, made a heartfelt promise to ensure that Ana would have a different path. She was determined to see that Ana would not be forced into an early marriage as she had been. Despite being convinced that God's will was what ruled life, Mamá Juanita believed in the importance of free will and believed Ana was entitled to opportunities and a chance at a different life. Ana had the desire to attend school and complete her education. However, when she reached the sixth grade, the demands of household chores and taking care of her seven younger siblings often kept her at home. Despite Mamá Juanita advocating for her aspirations, the practicality of the situation led Papá Lucho to decide that it was best for Ana not to continue attending school based on his belief that her assistance at home was more pressing.

Her older brother Jose Luis had dropped out of school during the fifth grade due also to Papá Lucho's need for help in tending to the farm animals and helping him harvest the fields.

Ana found herself shouldering the responsibility of helping my grandmother raise her younger siblings. She yearned for a life different from that of Mamá Juanita, one that went beyond serving a man and bearing children. Ana had aspirations and dreams that extended beyond the confines of her household and traditional gender roles. She wanted to pursue her own ambitions and create a life of independence and self-fulfillment. However, caught between her own desires and the expectations placed upon her made her feel that she did not have the right to choose her own path and seek a different life. As Ana's siblings grew into their teenage years and required less of her care, my grandmother arranged for her to become a seamstress. Doña Clementina, one of the few affluent women in El Romance, took Ana as an apprentice, teaching her sewing in exchange for her cleaning services. Ana despised working with Doña Clementina due to the lady's abusive behavior and the excessive workload she imposed. Driven by her dissatisfaction, Ana made the decision to pursue nursing instead. She began secretly volunteering for the Red Cross in a neighboring city, knowing that Papá Lucho would disapprove of her journeying alone to learn the nursing profession in another pueblo. To deceive Papá Lucho, Ana made him believe that she was at Doña Clementina's learning the art of sewing. Papá Lucho could never find out because he spent his days working the fields from sunrise to sunset.

As a Red Cross volunteer, she absorbed as much knowledge as she could. It was there that she started to contemplate migrating to the United States to pursue her nursing career. Growing up, she had seen many of the townspeople and neighbors move to El Norte in search of a better life. However, those families never returned, leaving their fate unknown. Once they left, nobody spoke of them again, as if they had vanished from the face of the earth. She spent a couple of years determined to overcome the financial and cultural obstacles that stood in her way to becoming a nurse. Unfortunately, as she approached her twenty-first birthday, the societal pressure to marry and have children began to haunt her. Women in her social circle bombarded her with fear-based and unsolicited comments:

"Ya estás en edad de casarte, Ana. Ya deberías de buscar un buen hombre. No te vaya a pasar lo que a tu tía Lupe que se quedó a vestir santos. La pobre, nunca sabrá lo que es tener un marido e hijos. ¿Y quién la va a cuidar de vieja? Mas vale que te apures."

While it was customary for young women in El Romance to marry at a young age, Ana wished to delay this. However, the social pressure weighed heavily upon her. When her younger sisters all married, people began questioning my grandparents about her choices. Her unmarried status defied societal norms. Hadn't they raised her correctly? Women neighbors often relayed the gossip they heard about her to my grandmother: "Juana, people are saying Ana is a *marimacha*."

Even the priest became involved, admonishing my grandmother during confession, "Juana, your duty is to guide your children. Ana should marry and have children. It is written in the Bible that women should be good wives and bear children. God's love should be manifested through her." Under the strain of societal expectations and the distress it caused her family, Ana found herself with no choice but to succumb to the pressure. She knew this burdened her parents deeply. Accepting the notion that marriage was the next step became her only option.

***

Dating in El Romance had evolved by the time my mother was ready to enter the courtship phase. Although it was frowned upon for a woman to be alone with a man who was not her brother, father, or husband, courtship was allowed under discreet circumstances, with no physical contact involved. The main plaza of El Romance served as the setting for these encounters. On Sunday afternoons, after attending Mass, men would gather at the four corners of the plaza. Women, accompanied by a friend or female relative, would walk around the plaza. If a man took an interest in a woman, he would approach her and ask if he could accompany her on her walk. If the woman reciprocated the interest, she would agree to be accompanied. However, if she was not interested, she would decline. If the woman accepted the company, they would walk side by side around the plaza, engaging in conversation. It was considered improper for a man to hold a woman's hand, with eye contact being the extent of physical contact allowed.

If the couple decided to become boyfriend and girlfriend, they could stroll through the plaza together, and he could accompany her home. However, the man had to leave her near her house to avoid being seen by neighbors. If a woman received a marriage proposal and she was certain, based solely on distant sightings and brief conversations without physical contact, that she wanted to marry that particular man, she would inform her parents. If her parents approved of the marriage, the couple would be granted a *plazo*, an additional period of time to openly get to know each other and determine if they truly wanted to marry. Plazos often lasted several months. At the end of the plazo, the man would bring his parents and a priest to the woman's home to formally ask for her hand in marriage. With the parents' and God's blessings, the wedding would proceed. I often heard stories from my mother and aunts about how their husbands courted them in secret, with each of them claiming that their husbands were the first men to hold their hands and kiss them. They emphasized that such intimacy was reserved for their wedding nights. While these tales seemed absurd to me, it brought solace to know that at least the women had the option to accept or decline courtship, unlike my grandmother Juanita.

Finding a suitable husband became Ana's focus. She walked around the plaza with a few potential suitors, but none met her expectations. She sought a man who embodied the traditional moral values she had been taught while also supporting her dreams of becoming a nurse. However, the men who courted her were often chauvinistic, refusing to accept that a woman could pursue anything other than domestic responsibilities. Others were known for their drinking habits or infidelity. As the months passed and the pressure to find a suitable husband intensified, Ana began to lose hope. One fall afternoon during the *fiestas patronales*, the town's festivities held to celebrate the patron saint of El Romance, San Judas Tadeo, Ana prepared herself to go to the plaza, hoping to find a potential suitor. The celebrations attracted many migrant men who returned to El Romance to participate in the festivities and traditions, expanding the pool of potential suitors, she thought.

Preparing for the fiestas and the search for a husband entailed several days of activities. First, she needed to buy a dress, but lacking funds, she had to make one herself. She sold a couple of chickens from their coop and several dozen ears of corn from their family's crop to gather enough money. With the funds she acquired, she purchased several yards of beautiful light blue satin fabric and crafted a simple yet stylish bouffant dress. To give it a touch of elegance, she added a piece of white lace fabric around the waist, resembling a belt. She also fashioned a choker from leftover lace. Unable to afford new shoes, she borrowed a pair from one of her married cousins whose husbands worked. By the start of the fiestas patronales, my mother had assembled the perfect outfit. She met up with two single friends, and together they made their way to the main plaza. They circled the plaza multiple times in search of promising suitors, but none caught her attention.

Feeling dejected, she chose to find solace on a nearby bench, where she could listen to the music and observe the festivities.

The rhythmic beats and infectious melodies of the *cumbia* song playing, filled the air, enticing Ana's body to move to the music. However, she hesitated, aware of the disapproving glances from older women who condemned a young woman dancing alone. Reluctantly, she suppressed her desire to dance and remained seated, longing for a miracle. She glanced toward the stage and spotted a man dressed in a cowboy outfit, sporting a long-sleeved denim shirt, denim pants, and a black Texan-style sombrero, slightly tilted. He was the lead singer, played the guitar, and danced with an unmatched passion. "It seemed like the music was emanating from the depths of his soul," my mother would later recount to me. Intrigued, she approached the stage, pretending not to notice the man. She was captivated by the man's robust physique and charming smile. He noticed her and immediately became enchanted by Ana's modest demeanor and conservative appearance. "It didn't take a minute before he started pursuing me," my mother used to boast when retelling the story. My father would always roll his eyes playfully.

Within a matter of weeks, they began dating, despite Papá Lucho's disapproval of my father due to his profession as a musician and his reputation for being constantly surrounded by groupies. Moreover, my father frequently traveled to neighboring towns and cities for performances and occasionally ventured to the United States. However, these obstacles didn't deter my mother. As soon as their plazo was over, they married. Shortly after their marriage, my mother became pregnant with my older brother Pedro. Overcome by the need for money, my father migrated to the United States to work, leaving my mother at the home of Mamá Cuca and Papá Merced. They didn't see each other again until a few days before Pedro's birth. My father stayed for several weeks until my mother recovered from labor, and then returned to the United States. For years, my parents' relationship was sustained through written letters. My mother dedicated herself to being a mother and wife and assisting Mamá

Cuca with chores. Mamá Cuca believed that a woman's duty was to her marriage and family, and that became my mother's life's purpose. Her dream of becoming a nurse had no chance given her circumstances.

CHAPTER 5

Travel to El Norte

M M   G   S   M A   . I R   O
my eyes. The dimness of dawn enveloped us. The distant crowing
of roosters echoed in the background. "Lucia, it's time, my dear.
Wake up," she whispered in my ear, planting a tender kiss on
my forehead. We had to catch the earliest bus heading north. I
quickly dressed in my white, ruffled dress adorned with knit,
knee-high, white socks and my black, patent leather shoes. My
mother carefully styled my hair into a ponytail, fastening it with
a white ribbon. This was one of the two special occasion outfits I
owned. The other, a blue dress lovingly knitted by Mamá Juanita,
was to remain safe at home, along with our other belongings.

We hurried out of the house, closing the heavy black metal
door behind us. Mamá Juanita and Papá Lucho were there to
bid us farewell. They stood solemnly beneath the blossoming
jacaranda tree that graced the front of our home. I could see my
grandmother's tears glistening on her weathered cheek as she
made the sign of the cross in our direction. Papá Lucho fought
back his own tears, silently witnessing our departure into an
uncertain destiny. Taking a few steps forward, I turned back one
last time to steal a glimpse of them standing beneath the fragrant
clusters of purple panicles hanging overhead. The purple blooms
seemed to droop, as if mourning alongside us on that day. Pressing
a kiss into my palm, I sent my grandparents one final gesture of
affection, just as a gentle breeze swirled through the air, carrying

away the fallen petals of the jacaranda tree and destiny propelling me farther away from my small town.

With only the clothes on our backs, we made our way to the bus station. I held onto my father's calloused hands, skipping in an attempt to match his hurried pace. Along the cobblestone street, we ventured toward the central plaza where the bus station was situated. As we reached our destination, my father entered the station and emerged with a bothersome expression. Anticipating a large investment in moving us to another city, he had purchase only three tickets, one each for himself, my mother, and Pedro. Leticia and I would have to take turns sitting on our parents' laps throughout the three-day journey.

It was July 4, 1991 when we boarded the old Tres Estrellas de Oro charter bus heading north. The charter had no air conditioner, and the inside felt suffocating. The seats were rigid, and sitting on my parents' laps for prolonged hours turned out to be agonizing. Passengers who couldn't afford seats stood in the aisle, further crowding the bus. Some passengers carried chickens and roosters in cages, making it difficult to maintain silence on the bus. The bus made stops at major cities throughout central and northern México. At each stop, people got on and off the bus, either to use the restroom or to continue their journeys. Street vendors briefly boarded the bus to sell typical Mexican snacks like fried pork skin, cut fruit seasoned with powdered chili and lemon, a variety of chips drenched in hot sauce, and a colorful array of peanut-based candy. Every time a vendor boarded the bus, my siblings and I would ask my parents to buy us a snack, but they couldn't afford to buy snacks every time. Instead, they encouraged us to get off the bus, stretch our legs, and breathe in the fresh air until we forgot about it.

Before embarking on our journey, it had been two years since I had last seen my father. He had returned just in time to celebrate my eighth birthday, and my gift was that he was taking us with him to El Norte. What I didn't know was that we were leaving

El Romance to migrate illegally to Los Angeles, California. All my father had told me was that we were moving to the beautiful City of Angels. Using our old Spanish encyclopedia at school, I had learned as much as I could about Los Angeles. I saw a picture depicting the Hollywood sign perched on a hill under a beautiful blue sky. Another picture showed the Santa Monica pier next to a vast ocean. I had started imagining myself living in the City of Angels. Although I had never seen the ocean in person, I imagined myself walking on the white sand, feeling its warmth and softness between my small toes. I envisioned our home with an ocean view, where the morning sun rays would enter through my window to wake me up.

We had been traveling for three full days when, near Mexicali, the air became humid, and the temperature unbearably hot. I had imagined a cheerful family road trip, but instead, the arduous journey was tedious and exhausting. My legs felt numb. With three hungry and agitated children and limited funds, the trip was a sacrifice for my parents as well. However, their determination to have a united family and a financially stable future kept them committed to that daunting bus ride. The sweltering heat had reached 105 degrees Fahrenheit, but an unexpected, sudden cool breeze wafted through the bus window, bringing me back to life. We were traversing the southern edge of the Sonoran Desert, gradually moving away from El Romance and closer to the US-México border. Excitement surged within me. I longed to escape the cramped bus, thrilled at the prospect of starting anew in a new city. Most importantly, I was overjoyed to finally be living with my father. I had missed him immensely during his prolonged absence from my young life.

***

After enduring three grueling days of travel, we finally arrived in the border city of Tijuana. During the second leg of our journey, we stayed at Aunt Esther's house. Aunt Esther was my father's first cousin, who, in her early twenties, had left El Romance with the intention of crossing into the US. However, while waiting at the border, she met and fell in love with a young man. They got married and settled in Tijuana, where Aunt Esther raised their five children on her own, as her husband turned out to be an alcoholic. She transformed her humble abode into a sanctuary for migrants, charging them a small fee for room and board while they awaited their turn to cross the border.

Aunt Esther's house was nestled on the hills of an impoverished neighborhood. It was a mixture of cement, cardboard, old wood, and rusted metal, giving it the appearance of a shack from afar. As we approached, a pack of dogs burst out of the house, barking incessantly. Following them, Aunt Esther emerged to greet us. She wore a traditional Mexican apron over a floral dress, her hair braided and secured in a bun with a hair clip. Her weary, dark brown eyes were trapped beneath wrinkled eyelids, and her light skin bore the marks of sun-induced dark spots. Yet, her smile was gentle and cheerful, as if she had not endured the hardships of raising five children on her own. Wiping her hands on the apron, she reached for my mother's hand, shaking it warmly before enveloping her in a loving embrace. She then proceeded to greet my sister, my brother, and me in the same affectionate manner.

"Welcome! I've been expecting you," she exclaimed, shaking my father's hand. "You've arrived at a good time. I heard from some coyotes that there hasn't been much migra activity in the past week."

"That's good news, Esther. We don't want to impose on you for too long. We understand how challenging it is for you, taking care of your own family," my father replied.

"Don't worry, Poncho. You know that my home, humble as it may be, welcomes anyone. I'm happy to help, especially when it's family," Aunt Esther reassured him. "Come inside. I'm sure you must be hungry. I've made fresh tortillas, refried beans, and *café de olla*."

"Thank you, Esther. You shouldn't have gone to the trouble," said my mother, expressing her gratitude.

"Don't worry, Ana. It's my pleasure. Only God knows when we'll see each other again. Once you make it to *el otro lado*, it could be years before a reunion is possible. Let's enjoy ourselves!" Aunt Esther exclaimed warmly, leading us inside to partake in the meal she had prepared.

I listened intently to the conversation between my father and Aunt Esther, though I didn't fully understand the gravity of their discussion. Meanwhile, Alicia and Adela, Aunt Esther's daughters, ran out of the house, catching my attention. Their bare feet were comfortable on the dirt floor. They wore flowery dresses and had long, untamed black hair partially covering their faces. Instantly, I formed a bond with the girls, as I had been a social butterfly from a young age. I ran off with them, noticing that Leticia seemed hesitant to join. She was shy and reserved, and it took her a while to warm up to new people and new situations. She clung to our mother's leg as she observed her surroundings.

Originally, my father had planned for us to stay with Aunt Esther for a few days, hoping for a swift border crossing. However, due to the implementation of new immigration laws under the George H. W. Bush administration, the number of legal immigrants had surged, leading to increased security and surveillance at the border. As a result, we had to remain in Tijuana until my father could find a trustworthy coyote who could safely and affordably take us across the border. Crossing a woman and three children illegally was a daunting task. It wasn't an easy decision for my father to entrust our lives to a smuggler. Aunt Esther recommended a coyote named Severino, vouching for his reliability and conviction to protect migrants during their journey.

That night, we met Severino at the nearest OXXO, a popular Mexican convenience store chain found on almost every corner. Severino was already waiting for us when we arrived. The bright red and yellow lights from the oversized OXXO sign illuminated his brown complexion. My mother and Pedro walked into the OXXO to buy milk and other provisions, while Leticia stayed with Aunt Esther. My father took my hand, and together we boarded Severino's 1980 Ford F-150 pickup truck, occupying the passenger seat. He briefly introduced himself.

"I'm Poncho. I was told you are one of the most trustworthy coyotes, Severino," my father said.

"I am. That's why my price is high. How many people?" Severino responded.

"One woman and three children," my father replied.

"Through *la linea* or *el cerro?*"

"Through la linea."

"One thousand dollars for the woman and two thousand dollars for each child. Cash. Fifty percent due when I pick them up, and fifty percent due when I drop them off in Los Angeles. No refunds," Severino stated matter-of-factly.

"You were recommended by my cousin. Is there any way you can—"

"I don't give discounts. Take it or leave it, amigo," Severino interrupted firmly.

My father took a deep breath, realizing the challenge of coming up with $7,000. With a shaky voice, he made the deal.

"When you have the money, call the number on this paper from a payphone. Simply say the number of people and mention OXXO on Avenida Revolución. They will tell you where to meet for payment and to discuss the plan. Now, get off the truck," Severino instructed.

We exited the truck, leaving Severino behind. The weight of the situation did not settle upon me as we made our way back to Aunt Esther's house. My young mind had no ability to comprehend that our uncertain journey was about to unfold. In my father's perspective, he was hiring a coyote to help reunite his family to give them a life of dignity in the US. However, in the eyes of the law, my father was about to commit a federal crime by hiring a human smuggler and conspiring to smuggle humans. Within minutes, my father had to make crucial decisions, such as whether he could trust Severino, the method of crossing and the price, which varied depending on the chosen method and destination. In our case, the plan was to cross through la linea, meaning we would be driven across the border in a vehicle through the designated port of entry, right under the watchful eyes of immigration officers. This was the most expensive option, as it entailed less risk and suffering for the *pollos*, the people being smuggled. Crossing through el cerro [the hills] was the least expensive but involved walking in a desert-like, arid landscape for several days, which was physically demanding and extremely dangerous. Crossing through the Rio Grande was also perilous, and my father, who had crossed through el cerro and the Rio Grande in the past, wouldn't dare subject us to such risks, even if it meant paying triple the price.

***

My father had a temporary work visa that allowed him to cross back and forth between the two countries. With my father having to return to California to work extra shifts and borrow money, we were left in Aunt Esther's care. Instead of a few days as planed, we spent a month in Tijuana. Our living conditions were far from ideal. My mother, Leticia, and I slept on a worn-out mattress on the floor, while Pedro slept on a dirty couch. Despite being only thirteen years old, Pedro took on the role of a guardian, always watching over my sister and me to keep us out of trouble, often encouraged by my mischievous nature. Life in Tijuana was especially difficult for my mother. To make ends meet, she started washing clothes for wealthier residents, struggling to earn some cash to feed us. She washed clothes by hand using a cement washboard, enduring immense physical strain. Since the house lacked running water, my mother had to carry buckets of water from the nearest well, which was about half a mile away. Pedro would accompany her, each of them carrying two full and heavy pails. On laundry days, my mother would wake up at five o'clock in the morning to fetch water and start washing. She aimed to finish by nine o'clock, allowing the clothes enough time to air-dry before the scorching afternoon sun. Windy days were especially troublesome, as the gusts would cover the washed clothes in dust, ruining my mother's hard work and jeopardizing her payment.

We had not anticipated staying in Tijuana for such an extended period, so we had brought no additional clothes with us. To make do, my siblings and I borrowed clothes from our cousins. It pained my mother to see us relying on others, knowing that our cousins also had limited clothing options. One day, Aunt Esther had an idea and took us to a large dumpster where affluent families disposed of their unwanted belongings. As we sifted through the dumpster, we discovered several plastic bags full of secondhand clothes in decent condition. Finding those clothes felt like stumbling upon a treasure.

The scarcity of resources extended to personal hygiene. Limited access to water and shampoo made it difficult for us to shower daily. As a result, Leticia and I became infested with lice. The sensation of the tiny insects crawling on our scalps and behind our ears was unbearable, causing constant itching. Under the scorching afternoon sun, my mother patiently sat, combing through our long hair, meticulously removing and killing the lice. Leticia and I cried as she pulled our hair, attempting to catch as many of the pests as possible. Eventually, realizing our ongoing suffering, my mother made the decision to cut our hair. It was the only way to eliminate the relentless insects. I cried even harder as I watched the strands of my beloved black hair fall to the floor. My mother hugged me tightly, reassuring me that it was the best way to rid us of the relentless infestation.

Despite the challenging circumstances, my siblings and I tried to make the most of our time in Tijuana. We found solace in playing under a massive eucalyptus tree on top of a hill, overlooking the city. From there, on clear days, we could catch a glimpse of the Pacific Ocean and the imposing steel fence that stretched for miles, dividing the two countries. Adela pointed it out to us, mentioning that once we crossed to the other side, we would never see each other again. I reassured her that we would visit, but she had seen many people leave and never return.

As the sun set and darkness enveloped Tijuana, we would run down the hill, our feet bare, my dusty skirt billowing in the fading sunlight, and my bald head making me feel lighter. I wore a joyful smile on my face. In those moments, we felt free and oblivious to the additional challenges that awaited us. We were unaware that this city marked our last stop before we became fugitives in a foreign land. We had no idea that soon we would be labeled aliens and forced to live in the shadows of a metropolis, hiding from the authorities.

***

The day came for us to embark on the final leg of our journey. My father arrived at dawn and woke me up, telling me it was time to get ready because we were going home. Sitting up on the old mattress, I rubbed the rheum from my eyes and threw my arms around my father, holding him tightly. He noticed my bald head and seemed shocked, but without saying a word, he kissed my forehead and handed me a plastic bag. Eagerly, I opened it to find the most beautiful outfit I had ever seen, even more stunning than my worn-out white dress and black patent leather shoes. It consisted of pink GAP shorts, a white top with a glittery "California" print, and pink LA Gear tennis shoes. After showering and dressing in our new outfits, my family was ready for the next stage of our journey.

Aunt Esther accompanied us as we left the house. My mother hugged her tightly, expressing deep gratitude for everything she had done for us. My father shook her hand, passing her a stack of bills, and she wished us luck. We walked three blocks to the main intersection and took a cab to the same OXXO convenience store where we had initially met Severino a month earlier. Within minutes of our arrival, a white Astro van pulled up. The driver was Severino. Stepping out of the van, he stood before us, tall and formidable at six feet two inches. His black hair was combed back, and his eyes were concealed behind dark sunglasses. A two-inch scar on his left cheek stood out against his acne-scarred face. He wore a collared shirt, jeans, and brand-name sneakers. He greeted my father with a handshake and nodded respectfully to my mother. Instructing us to get inside the van, he engaged in a brief conversation with my father.

"It's not the best day. The border patrol is on high alert today, but they've already met their quota by seizing several vehicles early in the morning. I'll see you on the other side in a few hours. Wait for us across the border at the McDonald's in Chula Vista."

Severino drove us to a beach and instructed us to memorize a new story about our identities and where we lived. He emphasized that my new name was Vanessa and that it was crucial for me to say we lived in Los Angeles with our family if questioned by an officer. We were to claim that we had gone to Playas de Tijuana for a day of fun. If asked, we were to say we were born at General Hospital in Los Angeles and were American citizens. Though the plan was for Leticia and me to hide under the back seats of the van until we crossed the immigration checkpoint, Severino wanted us to rehearse this story in case we were caught, detained, and questioned. He stressed that we must not come out under any circumstances until he instructed us to do so. My mother and brother would pretend to be Severino's wife and son, respectively. Severino had obtained counterfeit documentation for each of us in case of an emergency.

As Severino explained our new identities, I couldn't help but be captivated by the vast ocean before us. It was my first time seeing the ocean up close, and it filled me with excitement. That place, that moment, felt like an enchanted land. Looking north, I spotted the familiar dark fence that Adela had pointed out from the eucalyptus tree. I strained to see the top of the hill and the tree, but they were lost in a cloud of dark dust and smog.

Interrupting my thoughts, Severino asked me to repeat my new name and the story of my new identity. I complied effortlessly. We then reentered the white van, and by noon, in the first week of August 1991, I, an eight-year-old undocumented girl, found myself hiding beneath the seat of a white van, heading toward the land of the brave. We waited at the vehicle port of entry for two hours, cramped and achy, trying to stretch out in the confined space. I thought about the City of Angels we were moving to, and about the ocean. I curled up my small, numb body and endured the overwhelming van ride. As the summer heat intensified, we approached the inspection point at the Otay port of entry, mere feet away from the presence of the border patrol. Outside, officers scrutinized every vehicle with keen eyes, and their canines sniffed for drugs and illegal immigrants. Suddenly, a foreign language reached my ears through the open window, and curiosity began to wash over me. However, instinctively I made myself smaller under the van's seat, glancing at Leticia, who had fallen asleep beside me. Then, a voice startled my thoughts.

"Where are you coming from? Where are you headed? Please present your documents."

We were before the border patrol officers. I heard dogs barking close by. I closed my eyes, fear gripping me tightly. Suddenly, a warm sensation spread between my legs. Urine streamed down, completely soaking my new pink GAP shorts. My heart sank, and I curled up into an even tighter ball, waiting for the nerve-wracking encounter to end.

CHAPTER 6

City of Angels

My family and I arrived in the United States on a hot August afternoon in 1991. Within several miles of crossing the Otay inspection point, Severino erupted in excitement. "We made it! We crossed! Welcome to El Norte! "His laughter filled the van, breaking the ominous silence and waking Leticia. "The girls can come out now," he declared. Leticia and I crawled out from beneath the passenger seats. I felt a wave of relief wash over me as I made my way to the back seat. Kneeling on top, facing the window, I forgot that my shorts were wet. I was eager to catch a glimpse of what El Norte looked like. Before me stretched a vast highway, its dark gray asphalt marked with a yellow line that extended for miles into the distance. The sun was shining, and tall, slender palm trees lined the edge of the road. I noticed a plane flying unusually low and couldn't help but smile. It reminded me of my days in El Romance, when I used to climb the guava tree and occasionally spot a plane soaring overhead. Back then, I would shout, "Airplane! Airplane! Bring my dad back to me! "But now, I no longer needed to rely on wishes to bring my father. He was waiting for us at a McDonald's parking lot in Chula Vista.

Severino took the exit from the freeway, and as he pulled into the parking lot, I caught sight of my father through the window. He was dressed in his customary attire of worn-out jeans, cowboy shirt, and black leather ankle boots. I waved at him, and his smile stretched from cheek to cheek, revealing his crooked bottom teeth. Severino parked the van, and my father approached, opening the passenger door where my mother sat. She stepped out, wearing a sheepish smile. My father embraced her and planted a kiss on her forehead. My mother then moved to the back seat next to Pedro, while my father entered the van and sat down beside Severino. I was excited for the days ahead, now that my family was reunited.

***

We continued our journey on the freeway, and within miles, my attention was captured by the vastness of the Pacific Ocean, sitting in serene stillness. The cloudless sky above and the sunrays reflecting on the brilliant, blue surface of the ocean created a luminous mirror that sparkled beautifully across the horizon. It felt as if life itself had extended a warm welcome to me in this new land. While the ocean held my gaze, I also found joy in observing seagulls soaring in the distance and the clouds drifting by. Even the smooth asphalt road ahead seemed beautiful, much more so than the potholed roads of Tijuana and even the cobblestone streets of El Romance. I reclined on the back seat, savoring every moment of the journey until sleep overcame me.

My siblings and I awakened to the sound of my father's voice saying, "We have arrived." The house we were to call home was on Pierce Street. It was made with blue stucco and had a black roof. Its front yard featured a green lawn that extended to the sidewalk, enclosed by a chain-link fence. In the center of the lawn stood a large mulberry tree, which filled me with excitement, knowing I would climb it, just as I had done with the guava tree back in El Romance. I imagined Pedro, Leticia, and I playing and rolling on the grass. To the left of the house, there was a driveway. The main house consisted of one story, with a sizable accessory dwelling unit adjacent to it and a large garage in the backyard. A front porch welcomed us, adorned with several white plastic chairs and potted plants that occupied most of the space. We disembarked from the van and waited for my father to settle the payment with Severino. As the transaction concluded, a middle-aged, stout woman emerged. It was Aurora, the woman who rented and managed the house. Her waist-length curly hair, permed and dyed in a rich plum-red color, partially revealed her roots beneath her unkempt bangs. She appeared stern and discontent. Aurora had migrated from El Romance many years prior and had turned managing migrant homes into a business. She oversaw a total of three properties, but happened to live in the accessory dwelling unit of the house we were moving into. She collected rent from all the tenants, paid the bills, and took a cut for herself. Severino drove away, and Aurora approached us.

"Buenas tardes, Aurora. This is my family," my father greeted her.

She scrutinized us from head to toe, as if inspecting damaged merchandise, and remained silent. In unison, we all greeted her with a polite "Buenas tardes." The awkward silence persisted until my father broke it once again.

"As we agreed, they will take one of the beds in the big room. *Mi hijo* will sleep with me in the living room," he stated, pointing to Pedro. Aurora nodded and wordlessly retreated back into the house. "Ignore her; she's rather peculiar," my father reassured us as he walked toward the entrance, and we followed suit, like a flock of ducks.

The main entrance led to a spacious living room area with medium-sized windows that looked out onto the front yard. Beyond the living room was the kitchen with a breakfast bar and three refrigerators. Two wooden stools with ripped fabric stood in front of the breakfast bar. A door on the side of the kitchen led to a side patio. Across from the kitchen was a bedroom with a window providing a view of the front yard. It had its own bathroom and a large walk-in closet. A dark hallway with dirty, brown carpet led to the other two bedrooms, which were smaller than the master bedroom. These rooms could comfortably accommodate only a couple. Beyond the two smaller bedrooms was a large family room with large windows that offered a view of the spacious backyard and the garage. From the windows hung old, sunflower-print fabric curtains. Adjacent to the family room was another restroom. While the house appeared beautiful from the outside, the interior was dark, unkempt, and dated. However, I was thrilled to have an indoor restroom and not have to heat water before showering—it felt like an incredible luxury.

The house was one of many immigrant homes across Los Angeles. It served as the home for seven immigrant families, including my own. Families like ours shared living spaces to save on rent and utilities. All the families came from El Romance or nearby towns. In total, there were thirty people—adults and children—living in the house. My mother, Leticia, and I shared the family room—the biggest room in the house—with the women and children from three other families. Each family had a queen-size bed where the women and children slept. I shared a bed with my mother and Leticia. During the summers, I would often toss and turn throughout the stifling night, hoping not to disturb them. The space surrounding our beds was our only personal space, serving as both a closet and storage area. We kept our clothes, shoes, and personal belongings, which were minimal, under the bed or hung them on the walls. Pedro slept on a thin mattress on the living room floor, along with the adult men, including my father and other men who still had their families in México. During one of our first nights in the new home, the intense heat disrupted my sleep. I got up to drink water. As I switched on the lights, cockroaches scurried between the cracks of the old countertops and the laminate kitchen flooring, passing by my bare feet. I recoiled in disgust and decided to quietly return to the room, no longer concerned with quenching my thirst.

The initial allure of our new home gradually faded away. As we settled in, the daily morning routine on weekdays turned into a constant race. There was a race to use the restroom. While the men used a restroom in the garage, all the women and children shared the two restrooms in the house. Once inside, the rush to complete our personal business was tense. Knocks ensued, forcing us to have limited time of privacy. Fifteen or more people vying for one of the two restrooms felt like a game of tag.

Sharing the kitchen and one of the three refrigerators was extremely chaotic. Despite everything being labeled with people's names, arguments would often erupt over missing food. Sharing a kitchen with seven other women posed challenges for my mother, who had to navigate around their schedules to prepare meals. The women divided the household chores among themselves, and my mother often took on mopping and sweeping, considering Pedro, who slept on the living room floor. The constant disagreements between the women over chores and shared spaces created a tense environment. My mother, wanting to avoid conflict and the risk of eviction, distanced herself from the other women as much as possible. Renting a place of our own was financially out of reach, and my father had made it clear that it wasn't an option. Eventually, living in such cramped quarters with so many people made me feel trapped, and I found myself longing for our home in El Romance.

Frequent fights among the children in the house became commonplace. Leticia and I were among the three girls residing there, outnumbered by older boys, some of whom would bully us, taking advantage of our limited English proficiency. Pedro stepped in to defend us, risking reprimands from our mother, who stressed the importance of not causing trouble to avoid being kicked out. Completing homework was also challenging due to the lack of a comfortable and quiet environment. We often resorted to sitting on our bed to do our schoolwork. Since my mother did not speak English, she couldn't help us with our English homework. We struggled to keep up and fell behind in ESL courses for years. Seeing us struggle with our homework while she couldn't help caused my mother to feel helpless and guilty. *"Soy una inútil,"* I would hear her say often. I recall hearing her sobbing in the middle of the night not understanding her grief.

***

By the time I was in sixth grade, my father worked as a janitor in a garment factory during the day and played at random bars at night. His demanding schedule meant that I rarely had the chance to see him. My father was focused and driven by the desire to provide us with the basic necessities of life: food and shelter. Some months, when he did not have enough music gigs and money was short, our sustenance came from the local food bank, and our clothing consisted of second-hand items from thrift stores. However, my father taking on two jobs to support the family allowed my mother to stay at home and care for us, while also keeping us out of trouble. She dedicated herself to walking us to and from school, cooking, cleaning, and tending to our needs, neglecting herself. She often regretted the decision to move to the United States, contemplating a return to El Romance, even if it meant separating from my father and leaving our fate to destiny. Yet, her desire to keep our family together and provide us with a better future kept her resolute in staying. Despite being physically close to my father, we never spent quality time together. Experiences of playing at the park, traveling, going out to eat, visiting the fair, or having him read me bedtime stories were foreign to me.

As I grew older, I began to grasp the realities caused by our socioeconomic status through my own experiences. Residing in an economically impoverished neighborhood, in a cramped room alongside other families was not the worst part. Surrounded by violence and limited opportunities was. I witnessed the harsh realities of gang activity and substance abuse. Silent nights were often pierced by the sounds of sirens, as domestic disputes and drive-by incidents disrupted our sleep. Weekends were marked by house parties that frequently descended into fights between intoxicated men, who carried both inflated egos and broken spirits. After the altercations settled, the presence of a police helicopter would fill the sky, its wings whirring and its bright light intermittently illuminating the dark neighborhood. The sight and sound of it terrified me, reminding me of the dangers that surrounded us. Over the years, I witnessed friends and relatives succumb to the snares of gangs, drugs, alcoholism, and death. For the first five years, my only refuge was the overcrowded family room I shared with other families.

While my cousins in México faced traditional expectations of early marriage and housewife roles, I encountered a different reality. In my gang-ridden Los Angeles neighborhood, I was confronted with the expectation of falling into a life of crime or early pregnancy, perpetuating a cycle of poverty and limited prospects. It was clear that this land of opportunity, El Norte, held little enchantment for people like me. I had to navigate the challenges and uncertainties that came with my upbringing. The path ahead seemed bleak. Poverty, ignorance, and hopelessness set the stage for my coming of age. Trapped in a community plagued by adversity, I grew up.

CHAPTER 7

Survival

"DID HE FIRE ME?" MY FATHER ASKED.

"Yes, Apá."

"¡Qué hijo de su chingada madre!" my father yelled angrily. Although I didn't know how to console him, I tried.

"Don't worry, Apá. I'll work to help you," I assured him.

"Mija, you're just a young girl. You can't help me," he responded.

My father developed chronic foot pain and swelling from standing for long hours at work. He called in sick for the first time in his entire life and had asked me to assist him in calling his supervisor and translating for him. The conversation was swift and unsettling.

"Mr. Jones, I'm calling on behalf of my father who is here with me. He is sick and cannot go to work," I told the supervisor.

"Tell your father that if he's sick, he better not come back to work. He's fired! These lazy Mexicans. They're so entitled," I overheard the supervisor say before abruptly ending the call.

I chose not to share the supervisor's derogatory remarks with my father, as I couldn't bear to see the disappointment on his face. I felt utterly helpless witnessing my father injured and unemployed. He had been like a video game character, focused on surviving and ensuring that we survived with him. He had always been strong and seeing his spirit broken shattered me. I was angry and desired nothing but to help him. Although I was a teenager, something about that situation did not sit well with me, it felt utterly unfair.

In the weeks that followed, my father's condition worsened and the little savings he had dwindled. My mother had no choice but to find work. She worked as a housekeeper for a wealthy woman in Encino for a week. However, after getting on the wrong bus, getting lost on her way home, and ending up in skid row, she became terrified and quit the job. Eventually, she found employment as a housekeeper at a nearby motel, which paid very little and was physically demanding. She worked there for a year while my father recovered. I noticed a change in her demeanor. Having a job seemed to empower her, despite the exhaustion. Bringing home money gave her a sense of liberation. However, the guilt she felt for neglecting her role as a mother and wife became evident. "Do you think I'm a bad mother?" she asked me when other women in the house criticized her for working.

"Men are meant to work and provide for their families. Women should take care of the home, Ana. If you keep working, your children are going to stray away from your grip. Poncho should forbid you from working," they told her.

It wasn't long before the women's warnings became true. Pedro's school performance began to decline, and he started getting into trouble. Leticia was being bullied at school, and my mother often had to miss work to attend meetings with teachers and the principal. Leticia became quieter than usual. I took on the responsibility of cooking and taking care of the family since my father could barely walk due to his chronic pain. My mother was eventually terminated due to missing work often. The financial strain this put on our family led to frequent arguments between my parents. We had no choice but to apply for government assistance. It was uncomfortable for my parents, as they had never asked for help before and were aware of the stigma associated with seeking government aid. It took a lot of convincing for my parents to agree that we apply for food stamps.

One Monday morning, I accompanied my mother to the welfare office. By then, my English had reached an intermediate level, so it had become a regular practice for me to accompany my mother to various appointments and translate for her. I translated at Leticia's parent-teacher conferences, my father's doctor's appointments, and in transactional matters like the one we were facing that morning. I disliked translating because often it meant I had to miss school, but I was the unofficial family representative and had no choice but to fulfill my duty.

We woke up early to catch two buses to the nearest welfare office. My mother packed a *torta de huevo* for us to eat. We arrived around eight o'clock, and there were already about fifteen persons ahead of us. The majority were women who resembled my mother; the children, although younger than me, reminded me of myself. The office didn't open until nine o'clock, so we stood in line, braving the cold for an hour. When we entered the welfare office, we were assigned a number and seated in a large lobby with many other women and children.

When our turn came, we approached the social worker's window; she didn't speak Spanish, as we expected. I tried my best to translate; however, certain things were beyond my ability to comprehend and tension started building in the conversation. Things took a turn for the worse, and the social worker began raising her voice aggressively. She was unsympathetic and impatient. She harshly explained that we were missing my father's pay stubs and indicated that we would have to come back another day. Frustrated, my mother tried to intervene, but it turned out to be useless. I tried to explain to the worker how tedious and difficult the process to get there had been. However, she refused to listen and her voice grew louder, causing everyone to look toward us. I felt voiceless, powerless, and embarrassed. As I thought how the unfair termination of my father's employment had led to this, I became angry. A strong passion began to grow within me, fomenting my desire to be an advocate for my family and for others. Eventually, after several trips to the welfare office, we were successful in applying for and obtaining food stamps, which came as blessing given our dire financial situation.

During the period that my father was disabled, he received the news that Mamá Cuca and Papá Merced had passed away. Mamá Cuca passed first and, a month later, Papá Merced followed her. Their deaths came at a very pressing time for our family. We were still undocumented and waiting for our green cards to be issued. Our financial situation was precarious. Hence, we were unable to attend their funerals. My father succumbed to sadness being unable to be by their side. "*Soy un mal hijo,*" I heard him say. Unable to provide any word or support to him, I began to feel a strong duty to rescue him and my entire family from the unfortunate circumstances we lived in. It was a duty that became so ingrained in my mind, I couldn't ignore it.

After several months of being unemployed and mourning the deaths of his parents, my father recovered physically and was able to return to work. My mother convinced him that she could continue to do some work to help supplement our income. My father agreed to her working part-time and she began babysitting a few children from the neighborhood. With the additional income and government aid, my parents eventually built a small savings. This allowed us to move out on our own. Six years after arriving in the United States, we left the migrant home behind and moved into a single-bedroom converted garage. In that garage, Pedro and I transitioned into young adulthood and Leticia became a teenager.

***

Leaving the migrant home was an accomplishment, but shedding the toxic mentality instilled by the people within my environment remained a challenge. As my determination to pursue higher education grew, I often faced discouragement from my extended family. They lacked aspirations and hopes of breaking free from the status quo. At family gatherings, my aunts assured me that I was destined for a life with low expectations, just like my older cousins who had migrated to the States before me. During a family gathering, I first shared my desire of becoming a lawyer. I never forgot one of my *tías*' response: "You won't be able to become a lawyer, Lucia. Only people with money can study. How will you pay for it? Look at your cousin Chely, who wanted to become a police officer but ended up pregnant and a single mother. You should find a job that offers overtime so you can help your father."

My desire to prove her wrong fueled my motivation. However, although I chose not to believe the gaslighting tactics, they inevitably planted seeds of fear within me. Their words of negativity would creep into my mind and knock me down like a bowling ball striking pins. I couldn't blame them entirely; their limited view of life was shaped by their lack of education and socioeconomic status. Moreover, my neighborhood wasn't the type that produced lawyers. It was a predominantly Latino and Black neighborhood plagued by racial disputes, ignorance, and poverty.

Through my self-imposed determination to lift my family out of poverty and escape the confines of my neighborhood, my survival mode was activated. With no money, connections, or network, education was my only way out of this environment. However, even that seemed out of reach since my parents couldn't afford to pay for my college education. At the age of sixteen, I received my green card and was able to get a job. My first job as a cashier at a fast-food restaurant started while completing high school. I shadowed my father, working hard and going to school. I lost touch with Mamá Juanita. Even though my mother spoke to her over the phone regularly, I convinced myself that my relationship with Mamá Juanita, like many other memories from my childhood, were things of my past. My sole focus became to get into college and succeed financially to provide for my family.

As soon as I was able to, I became an American citizen. There was nothing else I thought that would get in my way of success. I had the drive, the legal status, and the need. I remained studious and focused. My mother's strict religious beliefs and my busy schedule kept me away from trouble. I did everything I could to save myself and my family, and be the role model that Leticia needed.

CHAPTER 8

Catholic Guilt

THE WARMTH OF THE SUMMER AFTERNOON EMBRACED US AS WE reveled in the grand *banda* and *norteño* music festival featuring the most popular Mexican bands of the 1990s that our local Spanish radio station organized. Banda and Norteño music resonated deeply within my community. Growing up, I developed a fondness for these genres of music, as they were the soundtracks to my family gatherings. This music coursed through my veins, their melodies and rhythms etched into my being. That weekend, Elena, my high school best friend, and I attended the festival together, with Pedro acting as our chaperone. We danced and sang joyously to "El Suase y La Palma" beneath the scorching rays of the Los Angeles summer sun.

Clad in my favorite jeans, cowgirl boots, and a *cinto piteado*, I felt the essence of a true banda and Norteño enthusiast. My pleated shirt was tied up above my waist, revealing my youthful and smooth stomach—a fashion statement embraced by young Mexican girls in my neighborhood. As we swayed to the music, executing the latest banda dance moves I had practiced in front of the mirror, I felt alive. Following the performance of banda El Recodo, Elena and I informed Pedro that we needed to use the restroom. While he cautioned us against getting lost and urged us to return promptly, Elena convinced me of venturing elsewhere. Hesitantly, I followed her as she giggled and laughed, leading the way. We evaded the dreaded porta-potties, disregarded Pedro's warnings, and made our way to the food stand instead. It was there, amidst the line of hungry festival-goers, that my path intertwined with Leonardo's.

As Leonardo approached the same food stand, our eyes met. It felt as though he had descended from the very essence of that summer sky. His deep green eyes held me captive, his disheveled black hair peeping out from under his sombrero, and his goatee perfectly framing his full lips. Wearing jeans, cowboy boots, and a fitted white *guayabera* that accentuated his slender figure, he embodied the epitome of a cowboy. My heart stirred with an inexplicable sensation. As he approached, I stood frozen in my own mocha-colored, uncomfortable skin, my black eyes widening with anticipation.

In the midst of our trance, Elena snapped me back to reality with a pinch. She whispered in my ear, "Lucia! You are being too obvious." Leonardo stood just inches away from me, and as if in a trance, we faced each other, exchanging smiles. Time seemed to momentarily pause, only to resume when Elena interjected.

"Good afternoon. My name is Elena, and she is Lucia."

"Lucia. A beautiful name. Doesn't it mean light?" Leonardo inquired, his hand extending in my direction as he locked eyes with me intensely. Nervously trembling, I felt myself getting lost in the depths of his captivating gaze and remained speechless. Elena, quick to notice my bewildered state, swiftly intervened.

"Yes, it does. Nice to meet you."

"May I buy you something to drink?" he asked, his words hanging in the air, filled with anticipation. Elena quickly interjected again.

"Yes, thank you, we will take an *horchata* and four tacos *al pastor* each." I had always admired Elena's audacity when it came to accepting guys' offers to buy us something. I could never do that. I could almost see my mother giving me a menacing look if I ever did this. However, I appreciated Elena's boldness, especially when we had just enough money to buy one drink each. Leonardo seemed pleased to stand in line with us and constantly looked at me flirtatiously. This was the first time a man had looked at me this way, and yet, my bashfulness seemed to dissipate as the desire to allow his charm to envelop me increased. After we got our tacos and horchata, Leonardo asked if he could hang out with us. I felt torn. Thoughts of Pedro and the fact that we had been gone for quite some time crossed my mind. I knew Pedro must have been searching for us, and it wouldn't be a good idea to keep him waiting. I hesitated, trying to come up with a polite way to decline.

"We're actually here with my brother," I explained, hoping to convey that our time was limited. "It's probably not the best idea for us to hang out longer."

But Leonardo seemed reluctant to let me go, and I didn't want to part ways with him either. There was a magnetic pull—a connection that I hadn't felt before. It was exhilarating and frightening all at once. Just as I was about to stand firm on my decision, Elena leaned in and whispered in my ear, insisting that we hang around a little longer and have Leonardo buy us *churros*. I couldn't believe her audacity. I shot her a judgmental look, hoping to convey my disapproval. She simply rolled her eyes at me, as if to say, "Live a little!" The desire to continue being in Leonardo's presence, to explore this newfound connection, swayed me. I took a deep breath, a moment of daringness overcoming my fear of getting caught by Pedro. I turned to Leonardo with a hint of a smile on my lips.

"All right, we can stay a bit longer," I conceded, my heart racing with a mixture of excitement and apprehension.

"Churros sound nice!" Elena said with satisfaction, knowing she had convinced me to seize this opportunity. As we ate our churros, Leonardo asked if there was a number where he could reach me. I hesitated, fully aware of my parents' strict prohibition against boys calling me. The thought of Leonardo calling our house filled me with apprehension, knowing that my mother would likely find out and severely reprimand me. I needed to find a way to see him again without arousing suspicion.

"Lady of Los Angeles Church," I blurted out, surprising Elena. "I go there every Sunday. I attend Mass at six o'clock in the morning and sit in the front row. You can find me there." Elena couldn't believe I had mustered the courage to provide such specific details. Normally, I was an incredibly shy girl when it came to matters of boys. Growing up in a conservative family had instilled in me timidity and fear of engaging in activities that other girls my age freely indulged in, such as flirting or having a boyfriend. My mother had employed Catholic guilt as a means of discipline, instilling in Leticia and me the belief that we were not allowed to have a boyfriend until we graduated from high school, which luckily for me was only a couple months away. The notion of sex had been shrouded in secrecy, only hinted at through passionate scenes shared by soap operas or gleaned from health class. Conversations about sex were strictly off-limits within our family. All we knew was that sex was considered a sin.

My mother had been raised in the same manner by Mamá Juanita, and her fear of God had only intensified when we moved to a big city and a more liberal society. I had listened to my mother and grandmother recount their love stories countless times, and in a way, I felt fortunate to have the freedom to choose my own husband. However, the absence of guidance regarding human expressions of love—touching, kissing, caressing, and ultimately, having sex—left me in a state of perpetual unease. I was simply told to avoid doing things that seemed wrong because God was always watching, ready to judge my every move. I lived in constant fear of sinning, unable to explore love in its purest form. The weight of Catholic guilt influenced my decision to remain celibate for longer than my peers. I feared the consequences of pregnancy, the shame it would bring upon my family, and the threat of eternal damnation.

The Sunday after Leonardo and I met, I went to Mass at six

in the morning with my family, as we had religiously done since I was a child. I had received Communion and was kneeling in prayer with my head bowed down when the thought of Leonardo creeped into my mind. Mass was almost over, and he had not shown up. Disappointment struck me as I stood and looked around the church, only to find he wasn't there. As my heart sank in disillusionment, my mind reminded me that there was always next Sunday. I sat back on the wooden bench waiting for the priest's blessing. I looked to the door for the tenth time, and to my surprise, standing by the entrance, was the tall, handsome man. A huge smile appeared on my face despite my attempt to remain in a state of contrition. He smiled back. All the emotions I had felt when I first saw him approaching me at the festival came back. My blood rushed to my face, my heart beat intensified. I was overcome with the desire to run to him and hug him. My mother noticed that I was distracted and looked toward the entrance to see what the cause of my distraction had been. Fortunately, she did not notice Leonardo and simply pinched me.

"Ouch! Mom! Why do you pinch me?" I whispered angrily.

"I'm watching you. Stop getting distracted. Pay attention. Consecration is the most sacred part of the Mass. You know that, Lucia," she said sternly.

I gave my mother an annoyed look, without her noticing of course. Otherwise, she would have fulminated me with her typical Mexican mother *vas a ver* look. She had been a good mother, but she had a way of disciplining us that included pinching, *chanclazos*, hair pulling, and stern looks; more than hurting our feelings, they scared us to death. I looked at Leonardo and noticed he was giggling. I realized that he had seen the whole spectacle with my mother, and I was deeply embarrassed. He winked at me from afar. As soon as Mass ended, I found an excuse to meet him. I told my mother I had to use the restroom. I walked toward the restroom and turned back to make sure my parents and siblings were not watching. I noticed they were distracted talking to other church members and catching up as they did every Sunday.

I went past the restroom, turned just behind the church's main building, and noticed Leonardo following right behind me. Within minutes, we were alone behind the church hall, standing in front of each other. Leonardo got very close to me. I trembled. As Leonardo leaned forward and took my hand, raising it to his lips for a gentle kiss, my heart skipped a beat. I could feel the warmth of his breath on my skin, and a rush of emotions coursed through me. The intimate gesture sent shivers down my spine. His actions felt like something out of a dream, something I had only read about in romantic Brontë novels or seen in movies. I looked into his eyes, still unable to fully comprehend the intensity of the connection between us. There was a mixture of tenderness and desire in his gaze, a silent affirmation of the feelings that had been growing within me. I mustered the courage to speak, my voice barely above a whisper.

"Leonardo, I didn't expect to see you here. I didn't see you during Mass."

He smiled, his eyes sparkling with mischief. "I couldn't stay away, Lucia. You have occupied my thoughts since the day we met. I couldn't resist the pull to see you again."

His words sent a surge of warmth through me, erasing any doubts or hesitations that lingered in my mind. In that moment, I felt a sense of freedom, of breaking away from the confines of my conservative upbringing. With a surge of boldness, I stepped closer to him, feeling the heat of his body against mine. I reached up, gently brushing my fingers against his cheek. The touch was electric, and a flicker of anticipation passed between us.

"I'm glad you came," I whispered, my voice filled with a mixture of longing and uncertainty.

"I want to get to know you, Lucia." He leaned in, his lips hovering just inches from mine.

"And I want to get to know you too, Leonardo."

In that secluded spot behind the church, in that fleeting moment, our lips met for the first time. It was my first kiss and though I felt an undeniable connection, a spark of possibility that held the promise of a young and pure love, I was terrified that he would notice my lack of experience. He insisted on speaking to me again that week and asked for my phone number. I reiterated that my parents did not allow me to talk to guys, so giving him my house phone number was not an option. He understood and promised to make it to Mass the following Sunday. Thrilled, I said goodbye and walked away before my parents noticed what I was up to. For the following two months, Leonardo, an non church-goer, forced himself to attend Mass every Sunday morning at six o'clock to get a brief glimpse of me. We found ways to spend more time together. He picked me up from school and dropped me off a block away from my home to avoid getting caught by my family.

My relationship with Leonardo took me on a complex journey where I had to navigate the intersection of love, desire, and religious beliefs. Leonardo had qualities that I admired: he was older, had a job and a car, and he was undeniably handsome. His romantic gestures and our shared moments made me feel like the luckiest girl in the world. But being raised in a devout Catholic family meant that I carried the weight of my upbringing and the teachings of my mother. I was constantly reminded of the expectations placed upon me; I was Leticia's role model. The Catholic guilt was a constant presence, looming over every decision I made. As our love grew deeper, Leonardo and I faced the challenge of our differing levels of experience and desires. While he respected my decision to wait until marriage to have sex, the intensity of our emotions and the desires within our young bodies became harder to contain. I struggled internally, torn between my love for him and the teachings that had been instilled in me since childhood. Throughout our relationship, I carried the heavy burden of suppressing my desires and maintaining my virginity. It was a difficult path, especially as I saw my peers embracing their own sexual experiences. They spoke openly about them, while I remained silent and distant. I fought to stay true to my values and aspirations, wanting to be the role model my younger sister needed me to be and not deviating from my path to become a professional.

As I approached eighteen, the struggle became even more intense. I yearned to experience that connection with Leonardo on a deeper, physical level. I confided in my friend Elena, seeking guidance from someone who had gone through a similar situation. She shared her own story and reassured me that any remorse she had initially felt after having sex had eventually dissipated. However, the cautionary tale of my cousin Lola's teenage pregnancy weighed heavily on my mind. Witnessing the shame and consequences that unfolded in her life, I became acutely aware of the potential risks of acting on my desires. I feared bringing shame upon my parents and jeopardizing my own dreams and aspirations. The fear of going against the teachings of the Church and the possibility of eternal damnation haunted me. For months, I grappled with this predicament, torn between my love for Leonardo and the fear of the potential consequences. In the end, I made the difficult decision to continue delaying physical intimacy until marriage. I clung to the hope that one day, when the time was right and our circumstances aligned, we could share that special bond even if it meant living in a constant internal struggle of longing and frustration. I held onto the belief that by staying true to my values and commitments, I was protecting my future and avoiding the potential hardships that could come with an out-of-wedlock, teenage pregnancy.

On my eighteenth birthday, Leonardo surprised me with a boat ride along the enchanting Venice Canals in Los Angeles. I had never ventured beyond my own neighborhood before, so the experience was completely new and magical. As we glided through the canals, the wind gently playing with my long skirt,

I felt a sense of freedom and excitement. Leonardo had prepared for the occasion, bringing roses and a bottle of champagne. We sat at the front of the gondola, surrounded by the picturesque scenery as the sun began its descent, casting a warm glow over the Pacific Ocean. It was a breathtaking moment, and my heart swelled with joy. Leonardo reached into his pocket and pulled out a small black box. My emotions soared as he got down on one knee and asked me to marry him. It felt like a scene straight out of the soap operas I used to watch, and I couldn't believe it was happening to me. Tears welled up in my eyes as a mixture of emotions flooded my heart. In that moment, though, alongside the overwhelming love and excitement, I also felt a surge of fear and apprehension. I knew that marrying at such a young age came with immense responsibilities and sacrifices. I had dreams of pursuing an education and building a career as a lawyer, breaking free from the traditional roles that women in my family had been confined to. As Leonardo patiently waited for my answer, I thought about the future I envisioned for myself. I wanted to do things differently, to carve my own path. And so, with a hesitant voice, I said, "Yes, I'll marry you, Leonardo, but you'll have to wait until I graduate from college."

The gondolier and Leonardo erupted with joy. The gondolier popped open the champagne, filling our glasses in celebration. It was my first taste of champagne, and the fizzy liquid made me feel a bit warm. I couldn't discern if it was the champagne itself, the whirlwind of emotions from the proposal, or my apprehensions about the future that unsettled my stomach. As the golden ring with a delicate diamond slipped onto my finger, Leonardo embraced me with tenderness and sealed the moment with a gentle kiss. The sun set over the City of Angels, and I couldn't help but wonder what the future held for us.

I kept my engagement to Leonardo a secret because I did not want my parents to be disappointed in my decision to marry at a young age. My parents had other hopes for me. They had hoped for me to become a professional and not a young wife and mother. As the weeks went by as Leonardo's fiancé, I had mixed feelings about my decision, yet it had been made. I was an engaged eighteen-year-old woman. However, the love and devotion that Leonardo showed me made me feel more at ease with my decision.

***

One evening, I sat on Leonardo's couch as he prepared dinner for me. I thought how different our dynamic was from my parents' relationship and the role I had seen men play in my own family. It was the first time I saw a man cook for and tend to a woman. The more attentive and loving he became, the more convinced I was that I had made the right choice in agreeing to marry him. We sat for dinner and he offered me a glass of wine. The idea that our married life would be like that moment made me desire it. I imagined him being a progressive and independent husband, who was loving and hands-on with house chores, and with whom I could build a family. I fell in love with the idea. I took my last sip of wine and leaned in to him. He kissed me tenderly and slowly; our kiss grew passionately. He began to caress my back. I allowed my emotions to overtake me. We stood up and he pulled me toward his erect body. Thinking I would marry him, I did not resist his hand slowly slipping down the depths of my warm, young abdomen and beyond. He began to untie my blouse and I willingly succumbed to my desire for his body. My blouse fell to the floor. He slowly pulled my skirt down and inspected my virgin body in awe. He wrapped his arms around me, picked me up and carried me to his bed. As he laid me on the mattress, he looked at me intensely and unloaded bursts of tender kisses on me, like a storm unloads mellow rain on a dry desert. I craved to stay under his spell. He whispered that he loved me and I allowed him to go farther within my body. My fears and my Catholic guilt melted away as his tongue found mine in the silence of my lips. I was suddenly transported to a magical place to which I had never been before. The electric shock of his fire ignited within the pureness of my heart. The thrill of the erotic moment drew me into a space without thoughts or expectations. I simply went and came like the current of a river, softly unwinding with a natural energy, allowing sacred water to flow from the depths of my body.

Later that night, back in the bedroom that I shared with Leticia, I was enveloped in adrenaline as I replayed the intimate moments with Leonardo in my head. My skin was still reacting at the thought of his lips kissing my inner thighs. I couldn't stop thinking about his naked body lying on top of mine, melting away in a union that I had never experienced before. I couldn't sleep reminiscing about the intensity and splendidness of our first sexual encounter. I do not recall what time it was when I finally fell asleep with the scent of his body on mine.

The next morning, as I opened my eyes and looked across at the wall, the first thing that I saw was an image of the Virgin of Guadalupe that my mother had given me when I turned thirteen. I remembered what I had done the night before and I broke down crying. I suddenly remembered my mother's constant warnings about staying pure until marriage. I covered my head with the pillow to prevent Leticia from hearing me sob. However, I mostly wanted to hide the shame and fear I felt at the thought that God and the Virgin had witnessed everything I had done. I felt like a fraud. I had let my parents down. I was certain I was going to go to hell. I refused to get out of bed that morning, unable to bear the weight of my dishonor. I could not comprehend how something so pure and beautiful could cause me to feel so awful about myself.

In the weeks that followed, the sermons in Mass were about sex before marriage. The priest said that it was a terrible sin that prevented one from receiving Communion. Every prayer seemed to say that I was a sinner who was not worthy of God's forgiveness. *No soy digna de que vengas a mi*, I recalled praying. Eventually, my sin weighed too heavily on me and I decided to confess. I thought that it would be like all the prior times I confessed when I was absolved of my sins because they never surpassed a mischievous act against Leticia or Pedro. However, when I told the priest my sin, he asked me if I regretted what I had done. I couldn't lie in confession, so I said that while I did regret it, I had enjoyed it. The priest gave me a judgmental look and asked if I would stop having sex with Leonardo. I knew in my heart that I could not. Hence, I was honest. He told me that he could not absolve me of my sin and that I would have to live in sin until we married. I left church in tears.

I had never imagined that falling in love and the Catholic guilt instilled in me would create a constant turmoil in my heart. I had never imagined that the emotions that are part of the human experience, like sexual arousal and the desire to fully embrace my sexuality, would come with shame and disappointment. I stopped confessing and receiving communion and when my mother noticed this, she outright questioned my attitude. I lied about my reasons for not confessing or receiving Communion, and this caused much tension between us. I spiraled into a state of shame that caused me much distress and inevitably to detach from my religion. I still went to church every Sunday, but I accepted I would live tormented until the day I married Leonardo, which I had promised myself would not happen until I graduated from college.

CHAPTER 9

A Whole New World

THE FALL AFTER MY HIGH SCHOOL GRADUATION, I ENROLLED IN community college. Although I had been considered a college-bound student and had the grades to attend a four-year university, my father reiterated to me on high school graduation day that he couldn't contribute financially. Years of working two jobs and getting only a few hours of sleep each night had taken a toll on him, making it impossible for him to work extra hours to support my college education. Nevertheless, I resolved to forge ahead and applied for financial aid. The process of applying for federal student aid was daunting, given my limited understanding of how loans, grants, and scholarships worked. Learning to distinguish the differences between each took some time and guidance from a financial aid counselor.

As if being a trailblazer in deciphering the college and financial aid application processes wasn't challenging enough, I also had to face criticism from some of my relatives for choosing to pursue college instead of finding a full-time job to help my father. They bombarded me with their limiting beliefs, unable to see a life beyond our gang-ridden neighborhood. Their convictions and indifference to my academic success were reinforced by their belief that life was about working hard, not wasting it on an education I couldn't afford. Their constant efforts to persuade me to settle for a life of low expectations instilled a sense of insecurity in me. On campus, I also encountered professors who attempted to extinguish my drive. In my first semester of college, a professor told me that he didn't think I belonged in his honors English class because I had graduated from a high school with a high dropout rate, implying that my chances of passing were slim to none. Throughout my journey in public education, I witnessed many of my peers in the same disadvantaged environment relinquish their aspirations due to the belief that higher education was beyond their grasp, given their economic class and ethnicity. Influenced by this, I gave up on the idea of becoming a lawyer. I opted for enrolling in vocational courses to become an administrative assistant. I had no one to turn to for advice. My first year of community college I was adrift like a leaf without direction.

After my first year in community college, I met a counselor, Mrs. Garcia, who recognized my potential, mentored me, and encouraged me to pursue my dream of becoming a lawyer. She helped me design a plan to transfer to a four-year university. The following years proved to be challenging. I took on two part-time jobs to support myself and pay for my education—a drive-thru cashier position at a fast-food restaurant and a cashier position at the campus cafeteria. I attended school full time and maintained a high-grade point average, all while maintaining my relationship with my fiancé. Despite just embarking on adult life, I worked tirelessly toward achieving my goal of attaining a profession, financial freedom, and advance socially.

My experience as a first-generation college student made me realize that I had to seize every opportunity available to me if I wanted to escape the cycle of low expectations and ignorance that surrounded me. Pedro had succumbed to our relatives' criticism and dropped out of high school to work at a factory and help our parents financially. This deeply saddened me, but I felt powerless to assist him. I was already swimming against the current on my own. Defying my relatives and taking on the challenge of becoming the first member of my family to attend college was a heavy burden to carry. Despite the limited guidance I received, I followed my heart. The perseverance and strong work ethic I inherited from my father propelled me to overcome the obstacles I faced.

As the semesters progressed, I found myself overwhelmed by the demands of work and school. Consequently, my relationship with Leonardo began to suffer. I had made a promise to myself not to marry him until I earned my degree. I wanted to be independent, self-sufficient, and to achieve a dream that no woman in my family had accomplished before. Making them proud was important to me. Leonardo started to resent me, feeling like he was no longer my priority. Although he wanted to be supportive, he worried that I was drifting away from him due to my focus on school and my dreams of becoming a lawyer. Arguments became frequent, and our bond started to crumble. I loved Leonardo, but I also yearned for the life experiences that higher education offered. I longed to transfer to a four-year institution, immerse myself in college life as depicted on TV shows, embark on adventures, and travel.

As my educational journey unfolded, I found that I had less in common with Leonardo. While he was hardworking and ambitious, he too was shaped by traditional Mexican values that assigned the role of provider to men and relegated women to caregiving at home. Although he had shed some of those beliefs, his lack of formal education limited his understanding of the experiences I was going through. I had so much I wanted to share with him, but he couldn't relate. I became confused about my feelings for him. I wanted to love him as intensely as I had when we first met, but I couldn't ignore the fact that my path seemed to be diverging from his. This inner conflict tormented me. I had compromised my religious beliefs and estranged myself from my faith to be with Leonardo, and now I questioned if I truly wanted to marry him. Naively, I feared that I wouldn't find another man who would accept the fact that I was no longer a virgin. Guilt and remorse plagued me as I completed my coursework at community college.

***

Two years into community college, I began the tedious and daunting college application process to continue to a four-year university. Once the applications were mailed, the long wait to obtain a response from colleges ensued. As winter arrived, I anxiously checked the mail, hoping to receive college acceptance letters. Initially I received denials from the Ivy league colleges I applied to crushing my ego. However, on a crisp winter afternoon, a large, fat envelope appeared in our rusty metal mailbox. As I pulled it out, the letters UCLA caught my eye, and my name was printed on the envelope. My body trembled with anticipation. I rushed into the house and tore the envelope open. The top page read, "Congratulations, you have been admitted to UCLA." After almost three years of arduous work and unwavering determination, I had been admitted to and awarded a full ride to UCLA, the university of my dreams.

I told my parents that I had been accepted to UCLA and that same day I also informed them that I was engaged to Leonardo. My parents had grown fond of him as he had been a gentleman and proved to love me. They loved that he was Mexican, and that his parents had raised him to be independent and hard working. My parents were proud of my choice in my future husband and my decision to continue with my education. However, when I told them I was moving to the dorms, they weren't so happy. They were accustomed to the idea that the women do not leave their homes until they get married. Hence, they struggled to understand the reason for my living away from home, especially when the university was an hour drive from our house. I explained that commuting would put a strain on my body and work and study schedule, and that living on campus provided me a more peaceful and quiet set up for studying. After much struggle, I convinced my parents it was best I moved into the UCLA dorms.

Preparing for the move to college brought a new experience. Three weeks before move in day, my mother, Leticia, and I took two buses to Los Callejones, LA's fashion district, to buy my college bedding set and other essentials. We walked through Santee Alley in the heat of the summer sun immersed in the shopping spree. I had picked up extra shifts at my fast-food restaurant job, and with the savings I bought additional decorative pillows, a pink San Marcos blanket featuring a white unicorn, a couple of indoor plants, and other decor for my dorm. After several hours of shopping, we were starving. With the left-over money, I treated my mother and sister to lunch at a hot dog stand. We sat on worn-out, plastic stools under a colorful umbrella. We each ordered a bacon wrapped hot dog and toasted with horchata drinks to the special moment as the street vendor flipped the simmering links in hot oil. The excitement of entering this new phase of my life was beyond measure.

***

I moved into the UCLA dorms with my parent's and Leonardo's help. My assigned dorm was on the west side of Hedrick Hall. After passing the elevators, I located dorm number 88 on the right-hand side of the hall. The door was slightly ajar, so I knocked before entering. Inside, I was taken aback by the smallness of the room. It contained a set of bunk beds, a twin-size bed, three desks, and a tiny closet for each occupant's personal belongings. The space was too cramped for my parents and Leonardo to join me, so they resorted to helping me carry stuff from the car and waited in the parking lot. Fortunately, I was accustomed to living in tight quarters, so this wasn't entirely unfamiliar. As I was scrutinizing the room, another young woman interrupted my examination.

"Hello, I guess we're roommates? I'm Lauren," she said.

"Hello. Nice to meet you. I'm Lucia," I replied.

As my dorm life began, I found myself sharing the space with two roommates who came from different backgrounds. Lauren, a young Caucasian woman, made me nervous at first as it was my first personal relationship with a white person. However, as we chatted while settling into our beds, my nerves started to subside. Soon after, Natasha, a young Black woman, entered the room. Her presence brought me a sense of familiarity since I had previously had Black classmates in high school. After a while, I realized it was time to say goodbye to my parents and Leonardo. I walked back to the parking lot filled with a mix of emotions. I felt thrilled and excited for the future, but at the same time, it was the first time I would be separated from my parents since we had immigrated to the United States. We had always stuck together through thick and thin, and now I was venturing out on my own. My mother fought back tears, and my father, who had been raised with the belief that men don't cry, held back his emotions as he hugged me tightly. I clung to them, promising to visit often.

Then it was time to part ways with Leonardo. I wanted to love him more, but I couldn't deny the fire and desire for a prosperous and adventurous life that burned within me. Our embrace lasted longer than usual, and he kissed me, expressing his love and anticipation for our eventual marriage after the two years were over. His words troubled me, as I couldn't reciprocate the same level of love and commitment. I felt guilty for not feeling the same way. I assured him that I would call him as much as possible. As I turned away from Leonardo and walked toward Hedrick Hall, I felt a sense of liberation. I remembered the advice Mrs. Garcia had given me: "Walk in there like you own the place." With my chin held high, I entered the new world that had opened before me. I was about to embark on the stage of my life that I had longed for. I wanted my parents to notice my assured stride from afar. Their sacrifices had set me free, and I was flying into a new world to pursue everything they could not have.

CHAPTER 10

First Gen Traveler

IN THE FIRST WEEK OF DORM LIFE, I MADE MORE FRIENDS THAN I could have imagined. I was never alone, always having someone to talk to or study with, regardless of the hour. However, these people were different from me, representing diverse backgrounds and perspectives, offering opportunities to diversify and expand my network. When I craved solitude, I found solace in the hidden corners of Powell Library. There, I immersed myself in reading my assigned books and relishing in the process of deciphering and analyzing new concepts. I acquainted myself with inspiring authors. College enabled me to see beyond my own world and circumstances for the first time in my life.

During that first summer at UCLA, I seized the opportunity to participate in a study abroad program. The desire to travel had always been a dream of mine. Though I hesitated due to financial concerns and the potential distress it may cause my parents, I sought guidance from a counselor who helped me navigate the financial aid options available. I also took on extra work hours to save money, ensuring I had everything figured out before breaking the news to my parents. I was determined to embrace all the experiences that being at such a prestigious institution could offer me.

I still remember the day I broke the news to my parents. My father was speechless, and my mother was dismayed. They couldn't comprehend why I needed to go to Europe to study when

I could do the same at UCLA. I realized it would be extremely difficult for them to understand, so I made the decision to lie. I told them it was required. Although I felt guilty about deceiving them, I knew that revealing the truth would only result in their lack of support. Being the first in my family to attend college had always caused tension with my parents. They struggled to grasp and understand the new experiences I was having and the ones I longed to pursue. While they did support my education, their protective instincts often led them to question my choices and fear for my well-being. In those moments, I realized that sometimes it was necessary to withhold information from them to shield them from further distress. Although terrible, it was a decision made out of love, meant to spare them unnecessary worry.

The course of study I had chosen required that I spend a month in each of three countries: Spain, Italy, and France. The day arrived for me to embark on my journey to Europe. The excitement and anticipation coursed through my veins, mingled with a tinge of fear. It dawned on me that I'd be further separated from my entire family, on a different continent no less. It felt as though my inner child clung tightly to my mother's arms, reluctant to let go. Simultaneously, there was an undeniable longing for freedom and adventure, a burning desire to explore the world beyond the boundaries I had known. Pedro, Leticia, and my mother accompanied me to the airport, their presence offering both comfort and a bittersweet reminder of what I was leaving behind. Leonardo was not agreeable to my decision to study abroad, hence he refused to accompany me to the airport. Tears welled up in my eyes as I embraced my family tightly. My mother's concerned gaze met mine, but despite my own nervousness and fear, I assured her that I would be fine. I promised to call her often, seeking to alleviate her worries. Kissing my mother, Leticia, and Pedro goodbye, I took a deep breath and mustered the courage to step forward into the unknown. This was a journey unlike any other undertaken by a woman in my family.

I was going from living confined in my rough neighborhood to seeing the world I had only glimpsed in textbook photos and cherished dreams. As the plane roared down the runway, lifting off into the vast sky, I could feel my heart soar with exhilaration and trepidation. The familiar landscapes faded into the distance, replaced by the boundless possibilities that lay ahead.

***

I arrived in Madrid on a warm summer afternoon, filled with a mix of nerves and excitement. Checking into the colonial-style hotel situated at Plaza de Santa Ana, I couldn't wait to begin my adventure. As I entered my hotel room, my eyes were drawn to the large window overlooking the plaza. It was a breathtaking sight, reminiscent of a scene from a Charles Dickens novel. Couples strolled hand in hand, surrounded by lush trees and towering Victorian buildings, while the vibrant atmosphere of shops and cafes filled the air. Children joyfully chased pigeons, evoking memories of my own childhood in El Romance, where I too had chased pigeons in the main plaza of my town. In that moment, I yearned for my family to share this magnificent view with me, feeling a twinge of guilt for having an opportunity they could not even dream of. Thoughts of my mother and grandmother crossed my mind, knowing they would never get the change to travel this far. I couldn't help but wish that one day, Leticia and Pedro would also have the chance to experience this beauty. Gazing beyond the plaza, my eyes fixated on the distant dome of the Palacio Real, its grandeur captivating me. With the night approaching, I nestled into bed, surrounded by the enchanting ambiance of Madrid.

The following morning, eager to make a good impression on my host family, I woke up early. Amalia, Manolo, Carlos, and Carmen were scheduled to pick me up at eight o'clock for breakfast. As I stood punctually in the lobby, Carmen, a thirty-five-year-old woman with a light complexion and blonde hair,

was the first to greet me, planting two kisses on my cheek—
an unfamiliar greeting that caught me off guard. Back in my
hometown, people typically shook hands. Following suit, Carlos,
Manolo, and Amalia exchanged the same greeting. Although it
felt peculiar, I went along with it, not wanting to appear ignorant
of their customs. Carlos kindly offered to carry my luggage as
we set off, ready to embark on my month-long stay in Spain.
During breakfast, Amalia broke the silence, her words laced with
a Spanish accent: "Oye, Lucia, cuando vimos tu foto, pensamos
que eras negra. Pero luego leímos que eras mexicana, y por eso te
escogimos" ["Listen, Lucia, when we saw your photo, we thought
you were black. But then we read that you were Mexican, so that's
why we chose you"].

I was taken aback by Amalia's comment, marking the
beginning of our conversation and our relationship on such a
note. I didn't know how to react or what to say. My dark hair
and brown skin, something I had always been self-conscious about
growing up, suddenly became overly conspicuous among the
fair-skinned individuals I sat with. Was I supposed to feel pleased
that they liked me because I was Mexican and not black? It was
a perplexing situation, and given my limited life experiences, I
realized I might not be equipped to handle it. I was now alone
among people who were very different from me, and aside from
being the only Latina in class on occasion, this was the first time I
felt truly out of place. Despite my education pushing me out of my
comfort zone, deep inside, I was still naive. Uncertain of how to
respond, I relied on the values instilled in me by my conservative
upbringing—to respect my elders and avoid talking back, no
matter the circumstances. It was one of the tools I possessed
to navigate the real world. I mustered an uncomfortable smile,
my body tensing at the lingering impact of her words. Manolo,
perceptive of the tension, attempted to ease the situation.

"What Amalia meant is that we love México. We love Mexican
food." I played along, engaging in small talk and reinforcing the

greatness of Mexican cuisine. Less than twenty-four hours had passed since my arrival in this new world, and already, I felt a sense of not belonging. The longing for my family and my comfort zone intensified.

Despite the uncomfortable and unexpected start to my stay in Europe, I remained tolerant and open to having a memorable experience. I quickly familiarized myself with the streets of Madrid, navigating the city with ease. Spain's efficient rail system and a map became my trusted companions, whisking me away to various destinations. I forged friendships with locals who introduced me to museums and the trendiest bars and restaurants in Madrid. Indulging in *patatas bravas* and *paella* and savoring the rich flavors of Spanish cuisine became a delightful routine. I embarked on weekend getaways to different parts of Spain, exploring its diverse landscapes and cultures. I even joined a flamenco class, mastering the intricate use of castanets.

However, amidst the joyous moments, I also encountered controversial experiences. Europe, a beautiful continent, exposed me to instances of discrimination based on the color of my skin. On one occasion, a cashier followed me in every aisle at a supermarket, keeping a suspicious gaze on me. It dawned on me that this part of the world, and perhaps the world at large, was not so different from my experiences in the United States. Witnessing the pervasive presence of ignorance and discrimination on a global scale was a sobering realization. It was disheartening to see how these destructive forces affected societies worldwide and were not limited to my own homeland.

Nonetheless, amidst this darkness, I discovered the existence of profound beauty in the architecture, nature and countless individuals. My Spaniard professors and friends embraced me with kindness and warmth, demonstrating the better side of humanity. I encountered selfless souls who extended their helping hands when I was lost in the labyrinthine streets of Paris. Ascending the steps of the Eiffel Tower, walking through the ancient corridors of the Colosseum, admiring the Sistine Chapel, and sitting beside the Fontana di Trevi, devouring a *torta* on baguette bread due to my dwindling finances, I found beauty and freedom in every experience. Each step I took, every night spent away from my family, and every moment outside my comfort zone pushed me to grow and fend for myself. The journey instilled within me a sense of fortitude, allowing me to face the world with newfound confidence.

Living in Europe and traversing its diverse landscapes elevated my life to a new plane of existence. The experiences I gathered expanded my perspectives, broadened my horizons, and transformed me as an individual. I developed a deeper appreciation for the richness of different cultures, the power of human connection, and the wonders of the world. However, I also felt a deep longing for home. The familiar faces, the warmth of my family, the flavors of Mexican cuisine and the comfort of my Latino community were calling me back. When the day came to return to Los Angeles, I felt a bittersweet excitement. I was eager to see my loved ones again and share my adventures with them. But I also knew that a part of me would always remain in Europe. It had become a place where I had discovered parts of myself that I never knew existed.

As I reunited with my mother and siblings at LAX, tears of joy and relief streamed down my face. I held them tightly, grateful for the reunion. My mother touched my face with relief, knowing that I was safely at home. My father was working as usual and had not been able to take time off to accompany the rest of the family to welcome me back. Leonardo was also absent. The last time we spoke, he hung up on me when I shared my decision to stay an extra month to travel throughout Europe. Our relationship had become strained. He had changed and been unsupportive. I brushed aside my thoughts of him and focused on my family, especially my mother. Her sacrifices had paved the way for me to have these incredible experiences. As we rode home, I shared stories, trying my best to convey the beauty and wonder of the places I had visited.

Coming back to UCLA felt like a homecoming of its own. I settled back into the rhythm of college life. I brought back with me a broader perspective on the world. The challenges I faced while abroad had strengthened me, and more than ever, I was determined to become a lawyer. Throughout the rest of my college stay, I continued to explore new opportunities, both academically and personally. I joined clubs and organizations that aligned with my interests, volunteered in my community, and pursued internships that allowed me to apply my knowledge in real-world settings. I became more politically engaged, advocating for social justice issues that were close to my heart. As my desire to learn more grew, my relationship with Leonardo lost its intensity. Within a month of returning from Europe, I rescinded my promise to marry him. More than ever, I wanted to continue with my education. He was ready for marriage and a family, and I was not. I had just started to live and to see the world and this inevitably led to the end of our relationship.

As graduation approached, I reflected on my journey from El Romance to the halls of UCLA. It had been a challenging and transformative experience, one that shaped me into the person I had become. I felt a sense of gratitude for the opportunities I had been given and a responsibility to use my education to make a positive impact in my community. On the day of my graduation, my family beamed with pride as I walked across the stage to receive my diploma. It was a moment of triumph, not just for me but for all the sacrifices my family had made. Although I knew that the journey was far from over, the knowledge and experiences I gained at UCLA would guide me as I ventured into the next chapter of my life. I felt unstoppable, ready to do anything, even become a lawyer.

CHAPTER 11

Lawtina

My initial understanding of lawyers was based on limited perceptions. I associated their work with helping people in distress, financial stability, and a glamorous lifestyle. These impressions fueled my desire to become a lawyer. Lacking any guidance to pursue a career in law, after college graduation I joined a program that assisted underrepresented students of color in applying to law school. Through this program, I had the privilege of meeting lawyers of color who shared their personal journeys and triumphs. Their stories resembled mine. Their resilience and ability to overcome obstacles captivated me, inspiring me to embark on the same path.

In that program, I also learned that getting into law school is particularly complicated for minority applicants, from the expense of test prep courses to the cost of actually applying to schools. In addition, as a first generation college graduate student applying to law school, it was hard to know the ins and outs of the application process without having personal connections to people who could help guide me through the process. In this program, I first learned that I had to take the Law School Admission Test (LSAT). I also found out that the statistics indicated that Latinos generally scored lower than white test takers on this exam. Hence, prep courses for the LSAT were a critical piece of success, yet they were financially out of my reach due the elevated cost. Financial constraints prevented me from affording a tutor, so I relied on my own determination and resources. Despite the odds stacked against me, I persevered, dedicating myself to diligent study.

I also returned home to save on living expenses. However, this posed another obstacle: finding a quiet space to study. Sharing a cramped room with Leticia allowed minimal space for focus. In our Latino household, peace and quiet were elusive, with constant noise from the television airing soap operas or Spanish news, neighbors' loud music, and neighborhood dogs constantly barking. I sought solace in local coffee shops and public libraries. Often I sacrificed sleep to study late into the night when everyone was sleeping. Although the process felt lonely at times, I stayed the course believing these sacrifices were necessary for my future success.

As I faced the LSAT, my scores saw only marginal improvements after multiple attempts. Realizing that a significant improvement was unlikely, I took a chance and applied to law schools with my average score. I embarked on completing the lengthy applications, which became a demanding, unpaid job, further straining my limited finances. After submitting my many law school applications and waiting months for responses, despite my efforts, my dream school, UCLA, rejected me. This rejection shattered my ego, as I had been accustomed to achieving success in my educational journey thus far. As the deadline to accept offers from the schools that I had been admitted to approached, I found myself torn between the prospects of moving to unfamiliar states such as Utah, Colorado, Wisconsin, or Arizona. None of the schools offered scholarships or the diverse campus environment I desired. Ultimately, I chose the school with the highest ranking, even though it did not meet all my aspirations. While disappointment lingered, I refused to succumb to despair. Though it meant leaving behind the familiarity of home and embarking on a different path than I had envisioned, I resolved to take the opportunity.

***

By the end of the summer, I was off to law school in Colorado. My parents rented a van to help me move there. We loaded the van with my most important belongings, which was mostly clothes, shoes, cheap jewelry, my San Marcos blankets, some books, my laptop, and a few small pieces of furniture. My mother prepared a load of tortas and packed fruit, pan dulce, and other snacks for the road to cut on costs. As we traveled east, I sat beside my mother in the van, resting my head on her shoulder, cherishing the familiar comfort. I knew I would miss her tremendously, but I also recognized that this step in my journey was one I had to take alone. The mixture of emotions—excitement, fear, and resistance—swirled within me as we ventured farther east. Breaking the silence, Leticia acknowledged the significance of the moment.

"Apá, esta es la primera vez que viajamos todos juntos desde que cruzamos la frontera" ["Dad, this is the first time we have all traveled together since we crossed the border"].

"De veras, mija" ["That's right, daughter"]. Leticia was correct. It was the first time our family had embarked on a trip together since we crossed the border and migrated to the United States. The lack of transportation and financial constraints had limited our ability to travel as a family, making this experience all the more precious. My father had stopped driving years prior due to his struggle with sleep deprivation. My uncle had taught Pedro how to drive, and my father had helped him purchase an old 1987 Honda, which became our primary means of transportation. The financial constraints left no room for travel in our lives. Hence, this road trip marked a significant milestone, a departure from the limitations of our circumstances. I chose to embrace the journey and enjoy the scenery as we crossed the Arizona desert, savoring the tortas my mother had prepared.

Our musical preferences clashed as the hours traveling in the crammed van passed. Each of us advocated for our favorite genre. I suggested *cumbias*, Pedro favored *rancheras*, and Leticia leaned toward hip-hop or R&B. My father, indifferent to the music choice, simply complied with loading any CD we handed him into the van's stereo and immediately fell asleep. As the hours passed, my mother resorted to her customary practice of prayer, clutching her old black rosary in her right hand. The crucifix swayed with the van's movements, and a pang of guilt washed over me as I momentarily recalled how disconnected I had become from my religion. I believed in God, but I deeply struggled with the strict commandments of my religion, which seemed to challenge some of my newfound beliefs, like the normalcy of sex before marriage. My father's sudden snoring startled me back into the present moment.

***

We arrived in Colorado after twenty hours of travel. The beginning of my new life in law school came accompanied by the unexpected twist of events for my parents: my roommate was male. His name was Wilson and we had been introduced over email by a mutual friend. He was a third-year law student. As Pedro searched for the address, I nervously took in the sight of the tree-lined streets and the vibrant flowers adorning the sidewalks. This was going to be my home for the next three years. Eventually, we located the address and parked the van. Before we made our way out of the van, I broke the news to my family.

"Mom, Dad, my roommate, whom you are about to meet, is a man."

My mother blessed herself with the sign of the cross and said her usual "Jesus, Maria, y Jose" ["Jesus, Mary, and Joseph"], an expression she often used when in disbelief. "What do you mean you are going to live with a man by yourself Lucia?" she said in disbelief.

"Mom, it's okay, trust me. I will be fine. He is my longtime friend." I lied.

"Well, how come we have never met him?" she continued.

"Because he lives here."

I had failed to inform my parents about this living arrangement, fully aware that it would come as a shock to them. Despite my father's near-choking incident and my mother's habitual expression of astonishment, I stood my ground, explaining that this was the living arrangement that I had chosen and that they could either agree with it or not because I would do it regardless. As a first-generation Latina woman, I had come to understand that part of my journey involved educating my parents about debunking cultural beliefs and myths. Living with a male roommate as friends was one such myth. After a long and uncomfortable conversation, my entire family accompanied me to apartment 111. I knocked on the door and moments later, a bearded, dark-skinned young man opened it. This was the first time I met Wilson. Although I had been nervous about the living arrangement myself and his failure to keep my secret that I had just met him, the reassurances from our mutual friend put me at ease. Wilson, sporting black-rimmed glasses, greeted us with a warm smile and introduced himself. He politely invited us inside, engaged in small talk, and then showed me to my bedroom, considering our exhaustion from the long journey. He handed me an extra key and mentioned that he had to leave. Before departing, he made it clear that we should make ourselves at home and help ourselves to whatever was in the kitchen. Wilson kindly offered his apartment as accommodation for my family. Gratefully, I accepted the offer, allowing us to save on hotel costs. My whole family stood in silence trying to grapple with the shock of the occurrence.

As soon as Wilson left, my mother wasted no time in meticulously inspecting the kitchen. She expressed her observations about the lack of dishware and the abundance of canned food on the shelves. Meanwhile, my father, concerned about leaving me far away from home with a stranger, offered his protective advice. He urged me to call the police if Wilson disrespected me and assured me that he would personally come and handle the situation.

"Mija, if this Wilson guy disrespects you, please call the police, and then I will come myself and handle him."

"Ay, Apá, no pasa nada," I reassured my father and chuckled at his protective nature.

The following day, after my family had helped me settle in and had rested, they began their journey back to California. Before leaving, my father took the opportunity to question Wilson further, obtaining his contact information and emphasizing that I was not alone. Although I felt a tinge of embarrassment at my father's protective measures, Wilson's sense of humor allowed him to understand my father's concerns. He assured my father that he would be like another brother to me. As I hugged my family goodbye and watched them disappear from view, I closed the door behind me and retreated to my bedroom, overcome with emotions. The realization that I would be separated from my family for three years weighed heavily on me, and tears welled up in my eyes. Despite my gratitude for the opportunity that lay ahead, the prospect of being so far away from my loved ones overwhelmed me. I recalled how much I had missed them during my four months in Europe and acknowledged that this separation would be even more challenging. I couldn't simply drive to California or buy a plane ticket to see them due to budget constraints and the lack of a car. Exhausted and emotionally drained, I curled up on my air mattress, surrounded by unpacked belongings, and allowed myself to release my pent-up sadness through tears. With a deep breath and a tight hug of my pillow, I eventually fell asleep, knowing that I had to find the strength to organize my belongings and face the challenges that awaited me.

***

On the first day of law school, I found myself riding alongside Wilson in his blue Honda Civic. As we made our way to school, I couldn't help but be captivated by the beauty of Colorado. Despite the end of summer and the cooling weather, the warmth still lingered. Wilson had warned me about the less pleasant winter with its frequent snowstorms. The city itself was nestled at the base of the Rocky Mountains, their imposing presence visible even from a distance. The surroundings were lush and green, and the air felt clean and pure. As we turned into the law school's parking lot, my nerves began to take hold. Sensing my anxiety, Wilson reassured me with a pat on the back and kind words, assuring me that everything would be okay. Grateful for his support, I walked with him to my first class, feeling like a child on the first day of kindergarten. It was comforting to have Wilson by my side.

Entering the classroom, I deliberately avoided sitting in the front row, having heard stories about the challenges that awaited those who chose that spot. Instead, I chose a seat toward the back, hoping to blend into the background. As more students filled the room, I anxiously awaited the arrival of other Latino students. Were they running late? However, as the clock ticked closer to the start of class and the room filled to capacity, it dawned on me: I was the only Latino student in my class. This was a far cry from my undergraduate classes at UCLA, where I could disappear in the vastness of lecture halls filled with hundreds of students. In this small classroom, surrounded by individuals who seemed comfortable in their white skin, my brown skin stood out. There would be no chance of going unnoticed by the professor this time. I glanced at my class schedule and saw that I was in Torts class. What did that even mean? My mind immediately conjured thoughts of *tortas* (sandwiches), and I took a deep breath, trying to calm myself. I looked up and observed my classmates interacting with each other as if they had known each other for years. Did they? I wondered. Did I even belong here? Doubts began to creep into my mind, unsettling my sense of belonging.

My thoughts were abruptly interrupted as a tall, slim, white male in his fifties stormed into the classroom, forcefully slamming a thick, red hardcover book onto the desk. It resembled an encyclopedia book in size. It was Professor Smith, my Torts professor. He was dressed in hiking boots, jeans, and a polo shirt. The room fell silent as all eyes turned toward him.

"Ha-ha! Fresh meat!" he exclaimed. "This is a large class, ladies and gentlemen. Expect it to dwindle in size by the end of the semester. Some of you will not make it past this semester. Some of you will fail. Some of you will quit. Some of you will never become lawyers," the professor declared, lacking any sympathy. I froze in my seat, overwhelmed by fear and doubt. I felt completely out of place, and the professor's words only intensified my feelings of inadequacy. I seriously began to question whether I truly belonged there.

CHAPTER 12

Dandelion

I HAD HEARD HORROR STORIES ABOUT LAW SCHOOL. I HAD BEEN told that the system was designed to break students down and eliminate those who weren't cut out to be lawyers. My impression was that law school students were usually top graduates with high GPAs, strong LSAT scores, and compelling personal stories that impressed admissions officers. This was my competition. Despite being a solid student throughout my life, my fears and insecurities prevented me from realizing that I could take on the challenge. I worried that I wouldn't make it. Professor Smith's introduction traumatized me.

The amount of homework I received after the first week of classes was unlike anything I had experienced in college. I had to read and analyze an average of three cases for each of my five courses daily. Many of these cases seemed archaic because they were landmark cases with historical and legal significance, shaping the application of certain laws, particularly those concerning individual rights and liberties. Learning to analyze a case was a skill that came with trial and error. I had to break down the case, identify the relevant facts, the rule of law, the court's analysis and reasoning, and the court's holding, a process called IRAC. As someone with an ESL background, I had to put in twice the effort to understand the legal language and concepts that sometimes felt like reading Latin. In addition, I had to take notes, memorize laws, and prepare assignments for my legal writing class. The workload was overwhelming, and for the first time in my life, I began experiencing severe anxiety.

The imposter syndrome constantly haunted me, making me believe I wasn't cut out for law school.

Then there was the fear of being called on by professors at random and being subjected to the dreaded Socratic method. The Socratic method, named after the Greek philosopher Socrates, was supposed to foster dialogue between teachers and students by asking probing questions that encouraged critical thinking. However, the whole experience felt like torture. The professor would randomly call a student's name and grill him or her while the rest of us watched in dismay. Under such pressure, I couldn't think critically. I was already self-conscious about my brown skin and overwhelmed with the insecurities that come with being a first-generation law student. Being put on the spot and cross-examined by my professors was traumatic, and I became convinced that I was far behind my classmates.

As the weeks progressed, the absence of a reliable support system added to the difficulties. Wilson was my only friend, and I clung to him like a child to its mother. We spent a significant amount of time studying together. Despite our bond, I frequently felt homesick. Wilson recommended that I join a student club or organization to expand my social circle. Strangely enough, I felt a sense of shyness and nervousness when considering this option. However, I recognized that Wilson also required his personal space, and it was essential for me to avoid relying on him excessively. Consequently, I heeded his advice.

A couple of months into law school, I formed a friendship with Mirta, who was one of the few Latinas on campus. She was from Miami and came from a Cuban background. Alongside Mirta, I also became friends with Azar, an Iranian woman from Boston, and Tony, a Chicano from Calexico. The four of us represented the only minority presence within our law school class. We shared similar backgrounds, including being first-generation law students and coming from underprivileged upbringings. Through these commonalities, we forged a strong bond and became best friends throughout law school. We even established a study group to support each other academically.

I lacked the comprehensive support system I had encountered during my college years. Consequently, I had to navigate this new environment independently and seek the support I needed from these like-minded individuals who, like me, had triumphed over adversity to reach this point. We spent countless hours together in the library, studying diligently. In between study sessions, we would take breaks to walk in a nearby park, which offered moments of respite. Whenever one of us succumbed to stress and anxiety, the others were always there to provide assistance and support. Our bond of *hermandad* became the driving force that carried us through the semester and led us to face our first midterm exams with determination. Wilson was delighted to witness my journey of finding my own path in law school.

As the fall season arrived and the leaves on the trees began their vibrant transformation, a sense of calmness gradually enveloped me in law school. The extraordinary beauty brought about by the changing colors of the scenery provided a much-needed respite from the demanding life of a law student. The city transformed into a palette of red, orange, and yellow, creating a picturesque backdrop along with the magnificent Rockies. However, this seasonal shift also served as a reminder that final exams were drawing near. The looming thought of not passing a class had never crossed my mind until my first semester in law school. The consequences of failing became starkly apparent. If I didn't pass my classes, I would be placed on probation, jeopardizing my ability to return for the following semester. Additionally, the substantial sum of $150,000 that I had borrowed from the government, along with its significant interest rate, would essentially go to waste. The weight of stress, fear, and anxiety inevitably returned as I grappled with these potential outcomes.

For the next couple of months, it seemed as though I had taken up permanent residence in the library. Endless hours were spent studying alongside my dedicated crew. One day, Mirta arrived at the library looking visibly distressed, prompting me to inquire about her well-being.

"What's the matter?" I asked.

Mirta began to share her concerns with a troubled expression. "As I was walking here, I overheard Fletcher and his study group saying that his father, who is a lawyer, created comprehensive study plans to guarantee top grades in their finals."

Azar interjected, her voice filled with nervousness. "John mentioned to me that his uncle, who is a judge, gave him an insider's perspective on the exam content. Also, he has already memorized all the material for our Contracts class because his cousin, who recently graduated from law school, shared his outlines with him."

"I saw Nicole walking out of Professor Smith's office. She looked so confident and told me that Professor Smith assured her that she would do exceptionally well in the final because she had hired an expensive tutor," added Tony.

The stories shared by our privileged peers unsettled all of us. I sensed my friends' anxiety, and it soon permeated my own thoughts. Unlike our counterparts, we didn't have connections to lawyers or judges, and neither did we possess the financial means to afford private tutoring. Taking out additional loans to pay for tutors was not a viable option. We felt left out and ill-prepared for the upcoming finals. It seemed as though our peers had a significant advantage, while all we had was fear.

"Okay, guys, we cannot allow this to overwhelm us," I said, mustering determination. "We have something that is unique. We have discipline, resilience, and a willingness to put in the hard work. Instead of wasting our energy on panic, let's channel it into learning. Who's with me?" As I spoke, I noticed a brief but tangible shift in their expressions, as fear and anxiety momentarily melted away.

***

The day of my first law school final exam arrived, and as I opened the booklet and read the question, a wave of confusion washed over me. Despite reading it a second time, I couldn't grasp its meaning. I took a deep breath, attempting to gather my focus. My classmates around me were already typing away, while I struggled to comprehend the question. Dread consumed me. I looked through the window and saw the snow-covered grass outside the classroom. I had an overwhelming urge to run away from that place. Although I had drifted away from practicing Catholicism, I closed my eyes tightly and whispered a prayer called *La Magnífica*, taught to me by my Mamá Juanita. "Pray it in difficult situations," she had told me. Despite reciting it multiple times, uncertainty still lingered. The ticking clock intensified my apprehension, and with each passing minute, I regretted spending ten minutes in prayer. I typed relentlessly until the time ran out. When I looked up, I realized I was among the last three students remaining in the room. With a knot in my throat, I turned in my exam. Never before had I felt such insecurity as a student.

As I returned home that day, the weight of defeat clung to me, and tears streamed down my face. Wilson saw my dejected demeanor and knew it was not the right time to inquire about how the exam had gone. He understood that feeling all too well, having experienced it himself. He embraced me and kindly offered to make hot soup. Although I appreciated his gesture, I declined, knowing it would be canned soup and not the comforting *albondigas* soup my mother always prepared for me when I was feeling down. After expressing my gratitude for his offer, I retreated to my room, locking myself in. The sense of loneliness intensified, and I longed to be with my family back in my hometown. Law school, along with everything it entailed, had shattered my self-confidence. The vibrant, optimistic young woman who had left Los Angeles felt dead, much like the fallen leaves buried beneath the cold, white snow surrounding me.

Right before my last final exam, sleep eluded me. The excessive caffeine consumption to stay awake and focused had taken its toll. After studying until the early hours of the morning and only getting a few hours of sleep, I returned to campus to meet my study group for one final session. My head throbbed, and my body ached. The thought of giving up crossed my mind, but I reminded myself that this was my dream—the dream I had fought so hard to pursue. I arrived for my last exam of the semester with bags under my eyes and worsening eyesight from the past few months. Just one more exam, and I would be free. Taking my seat, waiting for the test to be handed out, I glanced around the room. My classmates appeared calm, and I realized how often I compared myself to them—a habit I despised. Frustration welled up within me, directed at them and at life itself. I took a deep breath, trying to clear my mind and focus. The exam began and continued, marked by moments of distress and a sense of not knowing what I was doing. Nevertheless, when I completed it, I rejoiced in knowing that my first semester of law school was over! The thought of going home for the holidays revived my spirits. I made a promise to myself not to think about my grades until after Christmas. Gathering my belongings, I rushed out of the classroom. I had already bid farewell to Mirta, Azar, and Tony the day before. There was nothing holding me back. I was done! Regardless of whether I passed or failed, I had made it to the end. I returned to my apartment, packed a small bag, and eagerly traveled to the airport to catch my red-eye flight from Denver to Los Angeles.

***

Pedro picked me up from the airport, thrilled to see me and wasting no time teasing me: "Ay, Lucia, ¿pos qué te panzo?" ["Hey, Lucia, what happened to you? You've gained weight"].

"Shut up, dummy. You have no idea what I have suffered," I retorted. Indeed, I had gained a significant amount of weight during my first semester of law school. I was unable to afford a gym membership, and the cold weather hindered outdoor exercise. Having just enough time to attend class and study, and no energy to work out, I had gained twenty pounds. Law school had consumed every ounce of my time and attention. While I was self-conscious about the weight gain, Pedro's teasing couldn't dampen my joy of being back home. I was ecstatic to see my parents and Leticia, and most of all, I was looking forward to savoring my mom's delectable cooking. As Pedro merged onto the northbound 405 freeway, toward my beloved LA neighborhood, a surge of happiness pulsed through my heart.

That winter break spent with my family was exquisite. The *pozole* and *tamales* my mother cooked restored my spirit. With every sip of *ponche* and *champurrado* I become alive. Sadly, the holiday season passed by like a rushing river, and as the first week of January arrived, so did my grades. I was filled with both terror and hope as I awaited the moment to check them. It was close to midnight when I finally mustered the courage to look at my grades online. As I scanned the list, my heart sank with each letter: "D, C-, D, C, C." I had never received a grade below an A in my life. I had studied harder than ever before, and yet those were the results staring back at me. I cried, overwhelmed by devastation and the desire to seek refuge in my mother's arms. With only a few days left before I had to return to law school for my second semester, I questioned whether it was even worth going back. Would I be placed on probation? What did that even entail? Unable to bear the weight of it all, I chose to attempt to sleep and push my dream of completing law school out of my mind.

The next morning, my mother noticed that something was amiss and asked me what was going on. "Lucia, daughter, what is wrong? Your eyes are red and swollen. Were you crying?"

"No, Mom," I said, avoiding eye contact with her.

"Come here, sit, and tell me what's wrong."

"I received my grades, Amá. I had never studied so hard in my life for such low grades. I got Cs and a D."

"Lucia, but that is not possible. You have been an A student since you were a child."

"I know, Amá. That is why I don't understand what happened. Amá, I do not want to go back to law school. I do not want to be a lawyer."

"Lucia, I do not think that is a good decision. You can be a lawyer."

"No, Amá, I do not belong there. Everyone is so different from me. Everything is cold and difficult. I miss living here, and no matter how much I study, I have only achieved mediocre results. Amá, maybe I am forcing this. Maybe I should do something else with my life. I do not want to go back."

I held my mother tightly, seeking solace in her warm embrace, and I cried uncontrollably. The weight of my disappointment and the overwhelming urge to drop out of law school consumed me. Professor Smith's words from the first day of class echoed in my mind, now making sense in light of my current predicament. I felt like an imposter, a complete fraud, and all I wanted was to hide away and never face the world again. My mother prepared a steaming bowl of my favorite *albondigas* soup, hoping to lift my spirits. The familiar aroma brought a fleeting sense of comfort. As I indulged in the savory flavors, my thoughts drifted to my friends Mirta, Azar, and Tony. I wondered how they fared with their grades, desperately hoping they had achieved better results than I did. It was as if they could read my mind because just then, a message notification flashed on my phone. It was Mirta, declaring her official decision to quit law school. Soon after,

I heard from Azar and Tony, and it seemed they had barely managed to pass. My heart sank for all of us, weighed down by our collective struggles. In that moment, a mix of disappointment and uncertainty enveloped me. Realizing that my friends were facing similar challenges brought a sense of camaraderie. However, I was determined to follow in Mirta's steps and drop out of law school.

As the day for my return to law school drew nearer, my mother approached me with a plea, her voice filled with hope. "Lucia, do it for me. Go back to law school for me." Her words resonated deep within my soul. While I understood the depth of her belief in me, I couldn't believe my mother had asked me to endure another semester for her sake. She had no idea of the immense hardships I had faced during my first semester. If only she knew the countless nights I went to bed hungry because the share of loan money for the semester had run out, or the painful falls I experienced in the snow as I trudged back to my apartment with a backpack full of heavy books after exhausting days of classes, or the moments of sleep-deprived delirium in the library. If she had witnessed these struggles, she wouldn't ask this of me. As my mother spoke, my father entered the house after a long day of work. The weariness etched across his face was undeniable. He appeared defeated, aged beyond his years. His once-dark hair had turned gray and thin, and a slight limp had crept into his walk. Removing his boots, he slumped onto the couch and immediately began snoring, exhausted. I glanced at my father, then turned to observe my mother. She, too, bore the marks of hardship. Deep wrinkles lined her forehead and mouth, and fatigue clung to her every feature. Age spots adorned her hands, and weariness emanated from her tired eyes.

In that moment, a profound realization washed over me. The sacrifices I had made in just one semester paled in comparison to the sacrifices my parents had made over the years to provide me with this opportunity. I rose from my chair and straightened myself, the weight of responsibility settling on my shoulders.

It became clear that my journey through law school and my pursuit of becoming a lawyer were no longer solely about my personal achievements or being on the honor roll every semester. It transcended those individual aspirations. It became a mission to grant my parents the financial freedom they deserved, to amplify the voices of others who, like them, had been marginalized, and to strive for social justice in their honor. The renewed sense of purpose filled me with a gust of fresh air. I realized that my path was intertwined with the hopes and dreams of my parents. With a resolute determination, I made up my mind. I would return to law school, not just for myself, but to honor the sacrifices of my parents and to dedicate my efforts to the pursuit of justice *por mi gente*. I looked at my mother and told her, "Amá. I am going to do it for you and for my dad. I am going to do it for people like us."

As I returned to Denver for my second semester of law school, a mix of emotions welled up inside me. Seeing Wilson, Azar, and Tony brought me comfort and a sense of excitement. However, when I saw Mirta, who had assured me she was dropping out, I was ecstatic. She had summoned the courage to continue on this challenging path too. It was a pleasant surprise to find that, despite the difficulties we had all faced, and that our class had in fact diminished in size as Professor Smith had predicted, our tight-knit crew was still standing strong.

As we embarked on our second semester, I felt a renewed sense of determination. I was committed to making the most of my time in law school. I knew there would be more challenges along the way, but with the support of my friends and the lessons I had learned from my first semester, I felt better equipped to face whatever lay ahead. Law school had tested me in ways I had never imagined, but it had also shown me the strength within myself and the resilience that comes from pursuing something meaningful. In my second year, Mirta and I started the Latino Law Society chapter in my school. Because our Latino student numbers were small, Azar stepped up to join the board despite not being Latina herself. Together, we sought to create a supportive community for underrepresented voices.

By the third year of law school, I discovered that legal research and writing were my strengths, and I wholeheartedly embraced them. However, I struggled with oral arguments due to my accent. Our Moot Court class's midterm was an oral argument in front of volunteer judges at the downtown courthouse. Determined to excel, I dedicated myself to rigorous preparation. Yet, there was one crucial detail I had overlooked completely: I didn't own a suit, and professional attire was mandatory for the oral argument. The realization hit me hard. I had never shopped for a suit before and had no idea where to start. Mirta, who was facing the same predicament, joined me on a shopping trip to the only mall we knew in the city. Our first stop was a chain department store. We made our way to the suit department, only to find a selection of frumpy and outdated options. Seeking assistance, we approached a store clerk who reluctantly brought out a few suits that were slightly more appealing. She handed me a size 10, but as I tried to put on the pants, it became evident that they wouldn't accommodate my figure. Requesting a larger size, we were met with disappointment. The store didn't carry sizes and styles that fit us properly.

For hours, we scoured the mall, desperately searching for suitable suits. Two days remained until the oral arguments, and our efforts seemed futile. The suits we encountered were simply not designed to accommodate our curves. Finally, exhausted from our search, we opted for purchasing our suits from a thrift store. I decided to defy the professors' recommendations to wear a skirt suit. Instead, I purchased a black, conservative pant suit that cost me $40.00. It was a deliberate act of defiance against the historical restrictions that had once denied women the right to wear pantsuits, and also it was a bargain. Mirta, on the other hand, refused to hide her hips and settled for a smaller-sized pantsuit, determined to make her presence and identity known. Although our shopping experience had been frustrating, we had found a way to adapt and assert our identities within the constraints of professional attire and the beauty of our curves. We were ready to face the oral arguments with confidence, knowing that our appearance and our accents did not define our abilities or the strength of our arguments.

On the day of our oral arguments, we entered the courthouse with confidence, dressed in our black pantsuits and matching black pump heels. As we climbed the stairs, a sudden ripping sound filled the air, causing Mirta and me to exchange panicked glances. Mirta's face displayed sheer terror as she asked me to check her back. To our dismay, her second-hand, size-smaller pantsuit had torn between her buttocks revealing her hot pink underwear. My friend froze and I needed to come up with a quick solution.

"It's okay Mirta. After I deliver my argument, I will meet you in the restroom and lend you my pants. I will stay in a restroom stall until you finish your argument and return them to me."

She could not answer, but her horrified look said it all.

"It's the only option, Mirta."

We had no other choice but to carry out this plan, so we did.

Once our oral arguments were complete, we hastily exited the courthouse. Mirta tied the jacket around her waist, trying to conceal the large hole in her pants. We found a bench just outside the courthouse. We both sat, took deep breaths, and removed our pump heels. Suddenly, as the adrenaline began to subside, uncontrollable laughter overcame us, the kind that shakes your stomach and brings tears to your eyes. Our journey through law school had taught us resourcefulness, and we were determined to leave our mark, no matter the challenges we encountered along the way, even in unexpected wardrobe malfunction situations.

I successfully completed law school in three years as originally planned. On the day of commencement, a warm Friday morning in June, the ceremony began at eleven o'clock. My family had made the road trip to Colorado to celebrate this milestone with me. As I walked into the courtyard, taking my seat next to Mirta, Azar, and Tony, a sense of awe washed over me. I had actually done it—I had completed law school! Reflecting on the arduous sacrifices I had made over those three years, from missing family gatherings to accumulating significant debt and putting my mind and body through tremendous stress, I felt a deep sense of pride. Gratitude for my family also enveloped me. They had been my unwavering motivation every step of the way.

Looking up at the sky, feeling the warm embrace of the spring sun, out of nowhere hundreds of dandelion seeds with their pappi gracefully drifting across the courtyard. They floated through the air, surrendered to the gentle breeze. In that moment, I saw myself as a dandelion, despite the hardships of law school, I was tenacious and had allowed myself to be carried forward by the winds of possibility.

CHAPTER 13

The Beast

I STOOD BEFORE THE MAJESTIC CATHOLIC CHURCH OF ST. ANDREW.
Its imposing façade, fashioned from time-worn stones, rose
majestically into the blue sky; its intricate carvings and elaborate
adornments told tales of both faith and history. The entrance,
guarded by two towering oak doors, bore crosses etched in
delicate patterns, while colorful stained-glass windows depicted
biblical scenes that danced with kaleidoscopic brilliance when
illuminated by the sun's tender rays. Each window seemed to
breathe life into sacred stories, mostly of sacrifice, suffering, and
faith. Through the wooden doors was the sacred space where
many had found strength and protection. It had been years since
I had walked through those doors seeking solace. I reached for the
heavy wooden door and opened it slowly, its creaking announcing
my hesitant entrance. A mixture of emotions overcame me as
I ventured inside. My footsteps echoed upon the white marble
floor, creating a reverent rhythm that resonated through the
vast space. The scent of incense lingered in the air, mingling
with the faint fragrance of aged wooden pews. I gazed upwards,
and my eyes were met by soaring vaulted ceilings that seemed
to touch the heavens themselves, reminding me of the limitless
nature of faith. I walked toward the ornate altar, a centerpiece of
devotion, standing at the far end of the church. It was adorned
with meticulously crafted religious artifacts and sacred symbols,
but the main character was an enormous crucifix that hung

from the ceiling and occupied the center. The flickering light of countless candles illuminated the altar, casting shadows that seemed to dance in homage to a higher power. The church was empty and quiet, and a sense of peacefulness emanated from all corners, offering a sanctuary of peace and reflection. Within the walls, generations of devout souls had sought refuge, guidance, and redemption through prayer.

I sat on the front pew trembling. My heart was a tempest of nerves and fractures. After years of being distant from religion and God, I did not know how to initiate my prayer. I knelt and did the sign of the cross. My eyes betrayed my rationality and I unleashed a storm of tears caused by the uncertainty, vulnerability, and profound sense of defeat I carried. I cried for several minutes, sniffling, and blowing my nose embarrassingly. Fortunately, no one was present to witness the episode. Crying helped and I was finally able to gather my thoughts. The soft glow of candlelight flickering in the distance felt like a warm welcome, encouraging me to pray and find solace amidst the turmoil. I thought of my mother and Mamá Juanita who had sought refuge in a church for years and, despite the harsh reality of life, had never lost faith. In that poignant moment of raw vulnerability, I yearned for their strong faith and guidance. I yearned for a chance to mend the fragments of my spirit, which had been shattered by failing the bar exam. I needed desperately to find a path toward believing in me.

I recalled my peers mentioning The Beast: the bar exam. Passing the bar was the last step in the journey to become a lawyer. Despite how horrible they made it seem, I went through law school thinking it would never be an issue for me. I figured it was like any other exam; I just had to study extremely hard for it. I made the decision to practice law in California, so I had to take California's rigorous examination. California's bar exam was renowned for being one of the most challenging bar exams in the country. Even prominent attorneys and politicians had either failed to pass or faced significant difficulties on their initial attempts at the bar exam. It was like a ferocious beast that only a select few could conquer. The statistics themselves told a daunting tale: a mere 26.8 percent of examinees had managed to pass the year I failed the exam.

I had survived the grueling three-day marathon, with testing taking place from nine o'clock in the morning until five o'clock in the evening, punctuated only by a one-hour lunch break between the morning and afternoon sessions. The exam encompassed six essay questions, 100 multiple-choice questions, and two performance tests. It was conducted in a vast exhibition hall where hundreds of students congregated to undertake the exam. Passing the bar exam was an absolute prerequisite for practicing law, a final hurdle that awaited me even after the arduous journey of law school. Determined not to underestimate its significance, I had taken out additional student loans to avoid any work commitments and dedicate myself entirely to studying. I rented a converted garage near my parents' home, where I could reside while focusing on exam preparation. I enrolled in a preparatory class, and dedicated my life for several months to studying. They were intense and isolated months, immersing myself in the memorization of countless legal concepts spanning seventeen different subject areas. Mastery of the IRAC (Issue, Rule, Application, Conclusion) method was paramount, but equally crucial was honing time management skills and developing mental resilience. I had poured hours of dedication and tireless effort into preparing for the exam. When the results were finally revealed, the realization of falling short shattered my spirit. The weight of expectations, both self-imposed and from others, felt like an anchor pulling me deeper into a sea of desolation. Feelings of inadequacy gnawed at my self-esteem, and the fear of disappointing my loved ones haunted my thoughts like a relentless specter. My confidence, once buoyant, lay fractured, and I questioned my own ability and worthiness to pursue my dream of becoming a lawyer once again.

The distress that enveloped me had brought me back to church and to God. This burden weighed heavily upon my shoulders and, since studying hard had not worked, I needed to regain my faith before taking the exam for the second time. I needed God to help me get rid of the immense burden of disappointment and self-doubt stemming from failure. I had lived tossed between waves of anxiety and fear as I replayed the moments of the examination and the results, each one etched in my memory with painful clarity.

The sacred ambiance of the church contrasted starkly with the turmoil inside me. For a moment, I wondered if there was a divine presence that might understand my pain and offer guidance. Willing to try anything, I knelt and began to pray the prayers I recalled from my childhood.

"Padre nuestro, que estas en Cielo, Santificado sea tu nombre, venga a nostros tu reino." I was unsure if such prayer could truly mend the wounds inflicted by failure, but I held onto a glimmer of hope that it might light the way toward repairing my self-esteem.

As I finished the prayer, I decided to just talk to God as if I was talking to a human. I sat there expressing my feelings and crying in between whispers. I let everything I carried in my soul—disappointment, fear, sadness, anger, everything—out. After being there for almost an hour, I began to contemplate the next steps, seeking strength to rise from the ashes of my failure and find the resilience to move forward. I'm not sure how, but I suddenly felt the motivation to get back on my feet and the confidence to take the exam one more time. I was grateful for the moment of respite and of feeling able to undertake that perilous trial once again.

As I walked out of the church, I reflected on my journey, convinced that I was closer than ever to becoming a lawyer and, with such a title, attaining a life of prosperity. Memories of my eighteen-year-old self resurfaced: the version of me brimming with motivation, passion, and idealism. That inner fire had propelled me forward. The demands of law school had disconnected me from the positive outlook I held during my childhood. I had further distanced me from attending church and practicing my religion, witnessing a loss of faith along the way. Furthermore, in the pursuit of a dream I believed would lead to happiness, I had neglected my physical well-being and personal needs. I had been broken down; although I had managed to rebuild myself, it felt as though my pieces were not reassembled in their proper alignment. Nonetheless, I was determined to try one more time.

***

The night prior to the exam, I checked into a hotel room near the convention center where the exam was to take place. On the exam day, I arrived an hour early, plagued by a sleepless night. Although I had retired to bed early, the typical bar exam nightmares prevented rest, keeping me awake for most of the night. I found myself sitting beneath a tree, eagerly awaiting entry into the expansive exhibition hall, which had been transformed into an assembly of countless tables and chairs, complete with a refreshment area offering water and coffee. I observed others still poring over their notes, and while I had brought mine along, the thought of revisiting them once more was unbearable. I felt sick to my stomach from relentless studying, yearning for the exam to be over. As I entered the examination hall, doubts surfaced once again. I questioned my readiness to compete against hundreds of fellow students in the quest to earn the privilege of affixing "esquire" to my name. Doubting myself and terrified, I nevertheless stood there, prepared to fight the final battle that would secure me a place at the table of attorneys.

The experience of taking the bar exam mirrored my first law school exam, but on a much more intense level. When I opened the exam booklet, the prompt seemed incomprehensible, immediately triggering anxiety. I had been advised to stay focused and avoid making eye contact with anyone, but the true significance of that advice became evident during the afternoon session of the first exam day. Three rows ahead of me, a fellow examinee collapsed, and paramedics swiftly intervened, rushing him out of the room. Glancing out of the corner of my eye, I noticed that everyone remained engrossed in their laptops, seemingly unaffected by the commotion. It felt surreal, as if the only thing that mattered was completing the exam. Caught up in these thoughts, I realized five minutes had passed. Determined to regain my focus, I disregarded the incident and redirected my attention to my laptop and the perplexing prompt before me.

On the second day, fatigue began to overwhelm me, and my neck and head throbbed with pain. I struggled through an entire day of 100 multiple-choice questions, each featuring lengthy and intricate hypothetical scenarios. By the third day, I felt like a zombie, yet somehow, I could still recall all the law I had memorized. However, the exam demanded more than regurgitating legal information. It required identifying legal issues, dissecting complex hypotheticals, analyzing them, and providing the best legal recommendations based on the given facts and the law.

I endured three days of grueling questions, doing the best I could. However, deep down, I knew that this exam demanded more than my best effort. Exhaustion had taken its toll, and my level of performance had not been optimal. Doubts crept into my mind. I questioned whether I had been deceiving myself about my ability to become a lawyer. I grew disillusioned with the system, feeling that it had been unjust and disproportionately difficult for me as a first-generation law student to reach this point. I understood that the exam did not define me or my capability to advocate for others, but in that moment, the test seemed detached from that reality. I had made tremendous sacrifices to sit in that chair, in that room, and take that exam, and yet all I wanted to do was escape. The third day came and went like a flash. At the end of it all, I was left feeling empty and exhausted. I slept for days.

***

The release of the bar exam results was scheduled just before Thanksgiving, and I couldn't help but find it cruel. If I passed, it would be an additional reason to be grateful during the holiday. However, if I failed, I would have to sit at the dinner table, overwhelmed with disappointment, dreading the prospect of going through the entire process once more. It seemed like an emotional challenge to try to maintain a sense of gratitude while feeling terrible about the results. Thirty minutes before the results were due to be announced at five-thirty in the evening, I found myself alone in the converted garage that I rented, seeking solace in my journal. I began to write.

> In thirty minutes, I will find out if I am a lawyer. It has been such a long journey. I have sacrificed so much and shed so many tears to reach my dream that it is unbelievable I am so close to reaching it. I trust that I passed the bar, but I cannot get rid of this feeling in my stomach that makes me want to vomit. I have been through so much to get to this day. I hope this is it.

The results came out at six o'clock. By five minutes past six, I was once again writing in in journal.

> My dreams have crumbled. My faith has been tested again. I feel like a failure. I feel embarrassed. My motivation and desire to become a lawyer have died.

I had failed the California bar exam a second time.

The snowball of emotions that overcame me the weeks following the results made my life feel like a daze. I felt in limbo, with absolutely no energy or desire to register for a third attempt to take the exam. Failing the bar exam a second time made me feel like a victim and brought about limiting beliefs. I felt that I was not prepared for the struggles that I had to overcome to become a lawyer and succeed in my career. I believed that gender-role socialization and cultural expectations about my role as a Latina woman, which had threatened my decision to pursue higher education, were true. I began to think that maybe my extended family and the professors who did not believe I could make it were correct in encouraging me to adhere to a more traditional female role, such as getting married and having children. I thought about the struggle to get to law school, including institutionalized discouragement. Throughout my journey in public education, I was discouraged by counselors and professors who had very low educational expectations for a Latina like me. They not only doubted my ability to be accepted to law school, but also blatantly discouraged me from pursuing a career in law, telling me it was almost impossible for someone like me to succeed in law school. When they realized I was determined to pursue a career in law despite their recommendations, they encouraged me to apply to less competitive schools or to pursue a more "traditional" career for women.

When I made it to law school, being one of only a handful of Latinx students in my law school class was cause for my accomplishments to be questioned. My admission to law school was often attributed to affirmative action benefits. Hence, I felt that I had to work extra hard to prove to my professors that I was there based on merit and ability. However, these erroneous perceptions caused me to experience self-doubt throughout my entire law school education. In addition, being a minority student caused me to feel lonely and alienated. My law school failed to provide mentoring opportunities to help me navigate my educational and career goals efficiently. I was unable to relate to most of my peers and I often felt that I did not fit in. Inevitably, this led to me having a negative experience in law school. Failing the bar along with these social barriers inevitably made me doubt my own ability to be a lawyer.

Within a few weeks of receiving the news of failing a second time, I found the drive to step into my local law school's library to start studying for the bar once again. Going through the bar exam for the first time had drained me physically, mentally, and emotionally. Facing the prospect of going through it again with a shattered spirit was a huge challenge. I felt utterly exhausted, with my self-esteem buried deep underground. Daily headaches and body aches plagued me, and nightmares of failing the exam tormented my sleep. Walking into the library, I expected to encounter familiar faces from my previous study sessions, but to my surprise, it was empty. The realization that I might be the only one who had failed struck me like a blow. I felt the urge to run away, overwhelmed by a sense of isolation. It appeared that life was playing a cruel joke on me. Was I the only one condemned to repeat this arduous process? Dragging my soul, I walked to the corner desk on the second floor where I had previously studied. Before I could open my laptop and books, I succumbed to tears.

Despite the sting of failure still fresh in my heart, by the end of the week I found a renewed zest of determination to confront the Beast head-on. Summoning courage from the memory of my moment in church after failing the first time, and everything that I been made to believe about my inability to become a lawyer, made me feel resolved to take the exam once more. I knew that the road ahead would be arduous, but not insurmountable. I already had the benefit of experience; having memorized the law in all seventeen subjects, I knew what to expect. I hung on to a flicker of hope to push me to rise from the depths of victimhood and disappointment.

Four months later, after enduring the same grueling journey, I found myself once again waiting for bar exam results. This time, the knot in my stomach was different. I had practiced more and studied harder than before. I had taken out an additional loan to afford a private tutor. I sought assistance from a therapist to manage my anxiety and fear. I had started exercising, finding solace in stress relief. I had turned to prayer, seeking guidance and strength. I reached out to Mamá Juanita, and she prayed over the phone with me. This time, I felt prepared to face whatever outcome came my way, determined not to beat myself up if I failed once more. Taking a few sips of wine and inhaling deeply, I logged into the State Bar of California website precisely at six o'clock. I finished my glass of wine in one gulp before gazing up at the ceiling. As the list of successful candidates appeared on the screen, I grabbed the mouse, my hand trembling. I scrolled down to the letter I: "Ingram, Irwin, Isaac...Inocencio...Inocencio, Lucia." My name was on the list! I screamed with joy, cheering in disbelief. Kneeling on the floor, I wept tears of gratitude. I conquered the Beast!

***

I had the earned privilege of being sworn in as a new attorney in an intimate ceremony that took place in my local court house. To my delight, my closest friends and immediate family were present. As I sat beside them, my gaze fell upon the California flag and the US flag standing proudly on the stage. Reflecting on my life's journey, I realized that the timeline I had once meticulously planned had taken unexpected turns, with detours, dips, and bumps along the way. Nevertheless, I had managed to find my way to the path I needed to tread. Then, I turned my attention to my parents. Their weary yet radiant faces exuded a profound sense of pride and joy. Moved by their presence, I stood up, raised my right hand, and began reciting the oath.

I, Lucia Inocencio, do solemnly swear that I will support and defend the Constitution of the United States and the constitution of the state of California against all enemies, foreign and domestic; that I will bear true faith and allegiance.

Each word reverberated in my heart, growing louder as they escaped my lips. Tears streamed down my face as I dedicated that moment to the women in my lineage and all the women who had paved the way for me in the legal field. It was a profound acknowledgment of their strength and resilience, but also of mine.

CHAPTER 14

Lost in Law Land

THE ALARM CLOCK WENT OFF AT 5:00 AM. I ROSE TO MY FEET AND did a happy dance. It was my first day on the job as a lawyer. I blasted cumbia music on my smart phone and jumped in the shower excitedly. As I scrubbed my body and lathered my hair with eucalyptus-infused shampoo, nervousness began to creep in. Nevertheless, I was eager to be a great lawyer and I was keen to learn everything there was to the profession. I hurried out of the shower, put on a brand-new white dress and a white blazer. I applied natural-looking makeup, and put my long, black hair in a bun. I put on my red pump heels and my gold hoop earrings and headed to my law firm.

A month after being sworn in as an attorney, I had unexpectedly received an offer for an associate position at one of the most prestigious national corporate law firms in the nation. The opportunity presented itself by chance. I hadn't graduated at the top of my class or attended a prestigious law school; however, destiny seemed to have intervened, placing an interview opportunity in my lap. Although I hadn't initially planned to pursue a career in a big law firm, I decided to seize the chance. The allure of being a respected lawyer and working for a renowned national firm captivated me. The salary offered was unmatched compared to smaller firms and non-profit organizations. I understood that it would require long hours and hard work. However, I had already experienced those demands during law school without the accompanying financial rewards. Thus, I embraced the opportunity. Young and motivated, I saw it as my pathway out of debt, poverty, and a means to secure a prosperous future for myself and my loved ones; my pathway to my American Dream. I held on to the belief that becoming a lawyer would bring me genuine happiness. I yearned to embody the idealized image of a lawyer portrayed on television, exuding confidence, donning impeccable suits, driving luxurious cars, and working from stunning offices in skyscrapers. That was what I desired and was going after.

I drove up to the high-rise office with a mix of excitement and self-consciousness. Despite my new suit and pump heels, my old, black, Honda stood out as the least impressive car in the parking lot. I brushed off the feeling, thinking that soon I would also have a nice car. I proceeded to the elevator, where I encountered the security guard. Eager to show that I belonged, I proudly presented my fob card, which confirmed my employment. The guard smiled and directed me to the second elevator, taking me up to the twentieth floor. The receptionist greeted me warmly and guided me to a spacious office with a breathtaking view of the downtown LA skyline. It felt surreal, like a scene from a lawyer's TV series where I was the protagonist. I wished my parents could have witnessed this moment. The glamour and allure of my new workplace was astonishing. Monetarily, guilt creeped in for not pursuing a job in the public interest sector to help individuals like myself and my family, as I had initially aspired to do. However, I saw it as an opportunity to pay off my student loans and to help my parents pay off our mortgage. Hence, I embraced that moment with a positive attitude.

***

Within a few months of being hired, I found myself working grueling twelve-hour days, seven days a week. I became entangled in a race to accumulate the most billable hours. I worked relentlessly, with my sights set on impressing my boss, earning a ten-thousand-dollar bonus, securing a raise, and positioning myself on the partnership track. Having two degrees and passing the bar exam seemed meaningless in the face of the expectations I encountered. I quickly understood that I had to work even harder to prove myself as the fierce and zealous attorney that my high-end corporate clients and supervisors expected me to be.

Work-life balance became virtually non-existent as I found myself consumed by work. I felt overwhelmed, constantly putting out fires throughout the day. While my mentor, a forty-five-year-old white, male attorney attempted to provide support and camaraderie, I could not relate to him on a personal level. Unfortunately, finding such mentorship within my firm proved impossible, as women and minorities were underrepresented in the world of big law. Eight months into my job, a male partner asked me to assist him with one of his cases. I eagerly took on the challenge. After spending considerable time conducting research and writing a memorandum, I presented it to him, hoping to impress him. He threw the document into a basket next to his desk, dismissively stating that he would get to it later. A couple of days later, he came into my office and callously tossed the document onto my desk, pages scattering across the room.

"Did they teach you anything in law school?" he asked sarcastically.

I froze and focused solely on the paper on the floor. The document was covered in red ink. He walked out of my office without offering any constructive feedback or comments, leaving me confused and disheartened. I felt as though I had failed a law school exam, and tears welled up in my eyes. I questioned whether I was cut out for such a competitive and stressful environment. However, I attempted to conceal my insecurities by relying on my ego. I closed the door to my luxurious office, putting on a facade of being robotic and invincible. I took on every case and project assigned to me despite my large case load. I simply worked harder and longer hours convincing myself that I would figure out a system to catch up. I refused to show weakness and dwelled on the derived sense of satisfaction from entering conference rooms filled with abundant food during staff meetings and dining at upscale restaurants with colleagues and clients. I sacrificed billable hours to attend expensive happy hours with partners and other associates on Friday evenings at LA's finest establishments, creating the illusion that everything was under control. I pretended to fit in with a group of individuals who appeared flawless in their suits, seemingly untouchable, relaxed, and almost godlike. I took pride in my six-figure salary, earning more money than my parents could have ever imagined. I found validation in being able to indulge my mother and sister with shopping sprees, reside in a luxurious beachfront apartment, drive a nice car, and wear stylish clothes. I convinced myself that I couldn't ask for more.

As the years passed, despite becoming a promising attorney, my daily routine left me feeling unfulfilled and devoid of any real accomplishments. My body grew larger, my hair began to fall out, and the constant tension and pain in my neck and back served as a reminder of the stress that consumed me. For a while, I resisted acknowledging that there was a problem in my life. I was suppressing my true feelings and grappling with the toll that my career was taking on my well-being and self-worth. The facade of success and material wealth couldn't fill the void created by a lack of fulfillment and a disconnect from my true aspirations. I felt guilty and ungrateful for desiring something different and considered myself fortunate to be in the position I was in, having made significant sacrifices to attain it. I made attempts to find gratitude in my job, recognizing that many law students would have considered it a dream job.

I focused on the personal growth I had experienced, building a strong character and becoming a zealous advocate. There was satisfaction in facing experienced opponents and standing up to formidable challenges. Winning motions against more experienced adversaries provided instant gratification, and eloquently arguing my position in front of a judge brought pride. Even completing my first trial, despite the loss and the blow to my ego, eventually evoked a deep sense of satisfaction. However, the notion of being on the partnership track evoked a sense of resistance within me—a feeling I couldn't fully explain.

When I sacrificed billable hours to visit my parents, it was uncomfortable to hear them proudly share with their friends that their daughter was an *abogada*—a lawyer. Despite the glamour and bragging rights that came with being an attorney at a prestigious firm, I felt a profound emptiness. My life felt imbalanced. I had allowed the pursuit of material success and societal validation to take precedence over my own well-being. The toll my job had exacted on my physical and mental health was undeniable and I found it difficult to share my parents' joy. I secretly yearned for a life where I could find meaning and purpose beyond the confines of a demanding corporate law firm. The realization that I needed to make a change and rediscover myself grew stronger with each passing year. The truth was that I had lost touch with myself and my own desires. I felt trapped in the golden cage of my career.

On a crisp November morning, I got ready for work as usual. I headed out the door at 6:00 am to make my 8:30 am hearing on the west side of town. On my way to the hearing, I received a call from my boss asking me to cover another hearing while I was there at that court house. I made a stop at my office to pick up the file sacrificing the short time I had to grab breakfast. I spent the morning juggling two hearings and several hostile opposing counsels. I rushed from one court room to another carrying a massive load of papers and files while trying to stay calm and collected dealing with demanding judges and hostile opponents. At 12:00 pm, I rushed out of court and got onto a jammed freeway heading to my afternoon deposition at my opposing counsel's office on the south side of town—another hour's drive. I had no time to stop for lunch, so I did a quick drive-thru stop and ate while I drove. When I got to the deposition and walked in the conference room the receptionist welcomed me.

"Good afternoon, are you the interpreter?" she asked as she looked at my dark hair and brown skin.

"I'm defense counsel," I said, annoyed.

It was not the first time someone assumed that because I was a woman of color, I was the interpreter, court reporter, translator, or even the plaintiff. While I tried to not let the comment get to me, the ignorant assumption never stopped bothering me. The deposition commenced at 2:00 pm. It was a heated one. My opposing counsel used unprofessional tactics to delay the process and my client's right to discovery the entire time. Heated arguments ensued on and off. At 4:30 pm, he ordered the court reporter to go off the record without my agreement.

"We are ending because I do not work past 5:00 p.m.," he said arrogantly.

"Counselor, I am not done asking questions."

"Schedule a second volume," he said coldly.

"You are obstructing my client's rights to discovery," I said in a frustrated voice.

"You know, I've been doing this much longer than you have, and I can assure you, no judge will side with you. It's over," he said patronizingly.

Another argument ensued and, despite my useless attempts to reason with him, he walked out of the conference room with his client at 5:00 pm. Frustrated, I made my way back to the office, fighting through the remainder of rush hour traffic. At 7:00 pm, exhausted, I entered my office. I still had four hours left to my day—four more billable hours to catch up on the pile of mail on my desk and the countless emails sitting in my inbox. This was my daily routine.

On my sixth year as an attorney, I felt completely uncomfortable in my life and began to resist my fast-paced morning routine. My grueling four-hour commute, my racing thoughts while I avoided crazy drivers on the 405 freeway driving to court, the long hours at the office, the heated arguments with opposing counsel, my painful feet, bound in high heels while I walked from courtroom to courtroom appearing at various hearings simultaneously—everything in my life felt painful and undesirable. I dragged myself through the norm, feeling the need for change, wanting to escape it all—until I crashed. Then, it all forcefully ended: the job, the commute, the routine, and the billable hours.

***

I woke up in a hospital bed, giving what felt like my last breaths. As my body succumbed to weakness and dehydration and as my lungs struggled to fill up with air, I thought of the different forms of me that had been formed throughout the years: the undocumented immigrant, the brown college-bound kid, the first member of my family to graduate from college, the UCLA alumna, the Latina lawyer—all of the social titles I had acquired, which no longer mattered. At that moment, I felt more like a spirit than a human. A sense of readiness to die overcame me. As my body lay weak in a cold and desolate emergency room, I solemnly hoped there would be another lifetime for me to live a different kind of life. The doctor interrupted my thoughts as he walked into the room. I could see him only faintly between my half-open eyelids. The last thing I remembered him saying was, "We are going to give you one last shot of Albuterol. If this doesn't work, we will have to intubate you." Dehydrated and ready to let go of life and the idea of being anything but a lawyer, I took my last struggling breath, then I lost consciousness.

Hours later, when I woke up, I was alone in the emergency room. It took me a minute to realize that my oxygen mask was off and I was breathing on my own. I pressed the button to call the nurse, and within seconds, my male nurse walked into the room. He had been kind and extremely caring.

"You made it! The Albuterol worked, and your oxygen levels are back to normal! You really scared us last night," he exclaimed. "You had an asthma attack."

"But I have not had an asthma attack in years," I said, confused.

"Well, something triggered your asthma."

Dressed in a hospital gown, my hair up in a tangled bun, my brown skin pale, my face without makeup and partly covered by my black-rimmed glasses, I lay there, trying to make sense of everything that had happened and hoping this was an isolated incident.

As soon as I recovered, I returned to work. Due to being hospitalized for a couple days, I was behind on my work. As I entered my office, the weight of anxiety began to suffocate me when I saw the pile of new files sitting on my desk and the overflowing mail in my inbox. Anticipating an imminent anxiety attack, I shut the door behind me and took a seat in my comfortable leather chair. I gazed out the window, observing the city below and attempted to regain control of my breathing. But something within me shattered, and tears started to flow uncontrollably. I couldn't continue down this path. It was time to admit to myself that I couldn't go on like this.

A harsh truth overcame me—becoming a lawyer had been influenced by fear, my circumstances, and growing up in poverty while witnessing injustice. I had spent most of my life in survival mode, and that led me to choose a job that offered security, a way to compensate for the scarcity mentality that haunted me. I had lived constantly trying to control my life to avoid the low expectations that plagued my extended family and community. Being a lawyer had garnered approval from society and earned me respect, even from skeptical family members who doubted my potential to succeed. I felt the need to prove that as an immigrant,

I could achieve success in this country. But as the sun rose, casting its light on my worn reflection in the window, I saw an older, exhausted, and deeply unhappy version of myself. I had sacrificed so much to defend and represent faceless corporations who didn't even know my name. In that moment of clarity and self-reflection, sitting in my beautiful office, I realized that I had lost sight of the reasons that had initially driven me to pursue higher education. I had transformed into a different person and disconnected from my true self.

The realization hit me even harder as I recalled the hurdles of entering a predominantly white-male profession. "Latinas account for less than two percent of lawyers in the United States," I had read many times before. That statistic revealed more than a disproportionate lack of representation. It also revealed that I was in for a long and lonely ride, which it was. The lack of mentorship highly impacted my ability to succeed in such a competitive environment. At various times, a client had called me asking for advice and made sure to suggest I run the issue by my supervisor before I returned his call with an answer. It was evident that some clients viewed me as less qualified than my male attorney counterparts. Along with the negative perceptions of my ability to litigate a matter successfully, I had to deal with condescending treatment by opposing counsel. In a profession that valued billable hours more than mental and physical health, taking time off had the potential for having an adverse impact on advancing my career. Stories of mental breakdowns among lawyers in other departments circulated, but vulnerability and admitting struggle went against the very essence of being an attorney. We were expected to be strong, confident, and composed, constantly wearing the mask of ego. Yet, at some point there was a breaking point. I had reached that point. I broke. I was pushed to the brink of burnout and distress. I had to get rid of my ego and come to terms with the fact that Big Law, and possibly law itself, was not for me.

I made a resolute decision to release myself from the constant turmoil. I acknowledged that leaving behind a six-figure job, which had provided financial support to my family, was necessary to pursue what truly aligned with my heart's desires. The desire to escape my circumstances and the life I had built became as strong as the desire to leave behind the bus that had carried me to the US–México border and the cramped migrant home of my childhood. This time, however, I refused to remain lost in the belief that a career alone would define my happiness. After submitting my final billable hours that December, and receiving only a fraction of the hard-earned bonus due to bureaucratic bullshit, I made the decision to resign. Within a week of resigning, armed with only uncertainty and two pieces of luggage, I found myself on my way back to El Romance. My sole intention was to escape my reality and rediscover the essence of my being.

CHAPTER 15

In the Heart of México

THE FLIGHT LASTED THREE HOURS, AND I BARELY SLEPT. AS THE pilot's voice came over the intercom announcing our imminent landing, a wave of butterflies fluttered in my stomach. Peering through the window, I witnessed the gradual disappearance of the myriad faint lights below, gradually overshadowed by the rising sun on the horizon. Memories flooded my mind, harking back to the day my family and I bid farewell to that land and embarked on a journey toward a better future. My eight-year-old self seemed so distant, considering all the twists and turns life had thrown my way since then. Professionally, I had achieved much to be proud of, yet I felt an underlying discontent, an emptiness that I could not explain. As a thirty-three-year-old woman, unfulfilled in my career and dissatisfied with material possessions, I couldn't help but ponder if true happiness existed at all, and if anyone truly experienced it.

My gaze shifted toward the mountains, where in the distance, atop the Cerro del Cubilete, the faint silhouette of Cristo Rey stood, overlooking El Bajio. It felt as if the Cristo Himself was extending a warm welcome, beckoning me back to where it all began—El Romance. Abruptly, the plane made contact with the ground, followed by a smooth deceleration along the runway. We were instructed to disembark and make our way to the gate on foot. Amidst the crowd of *paisanos* (my fellow Mexicans returning home to reunite with their families for the holidays), I retrieved my carry-on luggage and slowly proceeded toward the plane's exit, my heart filled with a mix of anticipation and nostalgia.

Stepping off the plane, a crisp December morning greeted me with a gentle kiss of chill against my face. The nostalgic scent of rich earth and wild flowers filled my nostrils. Yet, it was the scent of burning wood that instantly whisked me away to Mamá Juanita's home. It was a place I cherished: the kitchen made of adobe bricks, where she skillfully crafted tortillas on the *fogón*. I would watch in awe as she effortlessly scooped a portion of masa, rolled it into a ball, pressed it onto the wooden press, carefully peeled the fresh round tortilla off the plastic, and placed it on the *comal* for heating. Despite my best attempts, I could never quite replicate her finesse in the art of making tortillas by hand. The challenge lay in flawlessly laying the tortilla flat on the *comal* without it breaking or folding. My grandmother, my mother, and Leticia possessed this mastery, and in our family, it was celebrated. Learning to make tortillas was akin to being ready for marriage, or so my aunts would jest. I found this notion absurd and eventually gave up my pursuit, resigning myself to savoring the delicious tortillas alongside refried beans, fresh cheese, and salsa made in *el molcajete*.

The morning fragrance of México enveloped my senses, intensifying my excitement at being back in my homeland. The brisk breeze nudged me to hasten my pace toward the arrival gate. Despite my parents' initial concern over my sudden decision to quit my well-paying, stable job and embark on a journey to México with no clear plan other than to escape my life, they had come to accept that questioning my choices was futile. My mother had arranged for my uncle Chepe to pick me up from the airport. I had made the decision to stay at a hotel rather than at our home in El Romance. The house had remained unoccupied for years and was no longer habitable. Besides, my plan was to spend just a few weeks in El Romance, returning to LA after Día de Reyes (Three Kings' Day). The thought of going back and facing the pressure of figuring out my next career move filled me with dread. The mere idea of working at another firm made my stomach churn, so I chose to tune the thoughts off and dedicate myself to finding Uncle Chepe.

Having not set foot in México for years, I wondered if I would recognize Uncle Chepe among the bustling crowd. As I made my way into the terminal, I found myself engulfed in a sea of people. Families clustered around the entrance gate, their eyes brimming with anticipation as they eagerly awaited the emergence of each passenger, burdened with their luggage. It was customary for paisanos to pay for extra baggage, which they filled to the brim with gifts for their loved ones. These gifts often comprised branded clothing, accessories, electronic gadgets, and toys that were more affordable and readily available in El Norte than in México. I had vivid memories of my Aunt Leonor, who had migrated to the United States long before my own family did. When she visited El Romance, she would arrive with suitcases overflowing with gifts for all her nieces and nephews. I recalled a particular occasion when she presented me with a necklace and bracelet adorned with imitation pearls. To me, they were more precious than any genuine jewelry. I reserved those accessories for special moments like my First Communion and birthday celebrations. The tradition of bringing gifts from El Norte had become deeply ingrained in our community, a tangible symbol of love and connection despite the physical distance. I was navigating through the multitude of families eagerly awaiting their loved ones when I heard a woman's voice exclaim with excitement, "¡Lucia! ¡Lucia! ¡Allí está! ¡Es Lucia!" I turned my gaze toward the voice and saw Uncle Chepe standing next to her. The woman was Aunt Matilde.

Overwhelmed with joy, I exclaimed, "¡Tía! ¡Tío! ¡Qué gusto verlos!" and rushed toward them, enveloping them in a heartfelt embrace. As I drew closer to my uncle and aunt, I couldn't help but notice how different they appeared from my memories. Their faces bore the marks of a life that had been anything but easy in El Romance. The deep wrinkles etched upon their skin spoke volumes of the hardships they had endured. However, despite it all, their eyes sparkled with genuine joy upon seeing me. My uncle's broad smile, even with a few missing teeth, radiated warmth that reached deep into my heart. We held each other in a tight embrace that stretched on for several minutes, cherishing the precious reunion.

Uncle Chepe, a taxi driver, was my mother's eldest brother. His upbringing had been marked by hardship and tough circumstances. As the oldest son, he carried the weight of responsibility for the family's well-being. At the tender age of seven, my grandfather entrusted him with the task of tending to the farm animals as they grazed in the fields. He was a young man when Papá Lucho fell seriously ill and became bedridden. Uncle Chepe received the solemn declaration that, as the male figure in the household, it was now his duty to work diligently in order to provide for my mother and their younger siblings. As a young adult, driven by a strong sense of obligation, Uncle Chepe made the decision to migrate to the United States in search of employment opportunities. Through sheer determination and diligent saving, he eventually acquired enough funds to purchase a taxi. Returning to El Romance, he wholeheartedly dedicated himself to his role as a cab driver.

His wife, Matílde, had endured a life of poverty and grueling work to raise their seven children. In order to supplement their income, she took on cooking and selling mouthwatering Mexican food outside their home on weekday nights, as well as doing laundry and ironing clothes for other townspeople on weekends. Despite their backbreaking labor and sacrifices to provide for their children, none of them had the opportunity to receive an education. Following the common pattern in El Romance, my cousins had married at young ages and started their own families. Despite the differences in our life paths, they were my family, and our shared heritage bound us together. Being in their presence made me feel at home, despite the years that had passed since our last meeting. The love I held for them only flourished as we drove away from the airport parking lot in my uncle's old Tsuru taxi toward El Romance.

Although my uncle insisted that I stay at their house, I hesitated to become a financial burden for them. Mexican families have a tendency to go to great lengths, even if it means spending money they don't have, to pamper their relatives visiting from El Norte. They'll purchase items they wouldn't typically buy for themselves—carnitas, *pollo rostizado*, and the family size Coca-Cola—all to demonstrate their deep appreciation and love for family. Furthermore, they refuse to accept a single peso in return. I always found this display of affection somewhat uncomfortable, but I respected their gesture. However, I didn't want to place my uncle and aunt in a precarious financial situation, so I made the decision to stay at a hotel instead, even when I knew they would take offense to my decision.

Before heading to the hotel, we made a stop for breakfast at the local *mercado*. My uncle and aunt suggested going to a nicer restaurant, but my heart yearned to revisit the places that held the fondest memories of my childhood. The mercado was one such place, where I wanted to relive the days of my childhood, running around with Pedro and Leticia while my mother shopped for groceries.

As we entered the mercado, my senses were immediately captivated by the vibrant sight of colorful *piñatas* hanging from the market stalls. The enticing aroma of fresh flowers filled the air. As we walked down the first aisle, the scent of homemade *chilaquiles* prompted me to a particular stand. Chilaquiles were one of my favorite traditional Mexican breakfast dishes. I adored the crispy corn tortillas, cut into triangles, lightly fried, and generously coated in red or green salsa. Opting for the green salsa, I requested extra fresh cheese and sour cream to accompany my meal. With each satisfying bite of chilaquiles and every sip of café de olla, I immersed myself in the lively ambiance as the market came alive with the bustling activity of merchants preparing for the day ahead. I made it a point to absorb every vibrant color, every enticing scent, and to behold every scene unfolding before me: the butchers arranging their meat, the cooks skillfully preparing their culinary delights, the fruit smoothie lady blending refreshing beverages, men pushing loaded dollies of produce, workers loading and unloading merchandise from large trucks, women diligently sweeping and setting up their stalls, and children hurriedly passing by in their impeccable school uniforms. These were the resilient Mexicans who had chosen to remain in El Romance, dedicating their lives to making a modest yet honorable living. They, too, had made sacrifices and toiled long hours to sustain themselves and their families, embracing the Mexican reality rather than pursuing the American Dream.

Around noon, following a satisfying breakfast and a leisurely stroll through the plaza, my aunt and uncle kindly accompanied me to La Casona, a reputable hotel in El Romance. They bid me farewell and assured me that they would check in on me later. I thanked them for their concern but insisted that it wasn't necessary. Once they were convinced that I would be fine, I proceeded to the hotel reception to complete the check-in process. As I checked in, a thought occurred to me, and I decided to upgrade my reservation, opting for a room with a balcony that overlooked the bustling plaza and the magnificent baroque-style temple across from it. It was a privilege to be able to afford this indulgence. In my childhood, staying in such a hotel had only been a distant dream. The view from the balcony offered a perspective I had never experienced before. It filled my heart with nostalgia as I recalled the numerous religious ceremonies held at that very temple, including Leticia's christening, my First Communion, Pedro's confirmation, and the weddings of many of our cousins. I closed my eyes, feeling a profound sense of gratitude for the beautiful moment. I couldn't help but wish that my mother could be there to witness it too. After settling in, I changed into the brand-new pair of huaraches that I had purchased at the mercado and I eagerly set out to explore the town's main square and immerse myself in the labyrinthine cobblestone streets of my beloved pueblo.

***

The following weekend, my family arranged a special gathering with all my extended family to welcome me back. The venue for the reunion was Mamá Juanita's home. I was overjoyed at the prospect of returning to the place I had cherished so much as a child, eager to reunite with the lush garden adorned with beautiful trees and flowers. I was also ecstatic to see my grandmother again. It had been many years since I had last seen her and I yearned to hug her. The weekend came and Uncle Chepe picked me up from La Casona. Upon arriving at Mamá Juanita's house, I was taken aback by what I saw. The garden I had known and loved was nowhere to be found, replaced instead by a plain cement floor surrounded by additional rooms and clutter. I immediately turned to my uncle, seeking an explanation for the absence of the garden. He shared that with all his children now married and starting their own families, they had needed to expand the house to accommodate everyone. In El Romance, it was customary for sons to bring their wives to live with their parents, while daughters would move into their husbands' families' homes upon marriage. With four married sons, Uncle Chepe had to construct additional rooms to accommodate his sons, their wives, and their growing number of children. My heart sank. I had envisioned myself sitting in the garden with Mamá Juanita and reliving the cherished memories of my childhood. I came to realize that many things in El Romance had changed, just as I had changed, and my family had changed. There were now countless cousins, nieces, and nephews who I had never had the chance to meet. After being over the shock of not seeing the garden, I proceeded to ask for Mamá Juanita.

"She cannot join us Lucia. She is a bit under the weather, and it is best that she does not expose herself," said Aunt Matilde.

"Can I see her in her room?" I persisted, determined to find my way to my grandmother's side. As I inquired about the whereabouts of her room among the numerous additions, a sudden hush fell over the air, and all eyes turned toward the back of the house, beyond the cement patio. I followed their gaze and was immediately captivated by what I saw. Slowly but eagerly, an elderly and fragile woman emerged, leaning on a cane as she navigated her way toward us with an antalgic gait. Her hair was braided into a long, white strand, and her blue *rebozo* partially covered her head. She wore a flowing white *huipil*, paired with huaraches. Despite the visible changes in her physical appearance since the last time I had laid eyes on her, there was an ethereal quality to her presence that instantly confirmed her identity as Mamá Juanita.

I rushed into her embrace, just as I had done countless times during my childhood. Standing before her, I was overwhelmed by a flood of emotions. Though her eyes were partially covered by pterygium, she looked at me with her beautiful black eyes and I immediately felt the profound love that she had shown me as a child. She reached out to me, and I melted into her bosom, finding solace in her presence.

"Lucia, mi niña," she whispered, her voice filled with tenderness.

As I clung to her, my voice cracked as I responded, "Abuela, aquí estoy." My tears streamed down, falling onto her rebozo.

"Sabía que vendrías, Lucia," she assured me gently, as if she had known all along that I would return. In that moment, a wave of guilt washed over me. I realized that I had neglected my grandmother all these years, failing to make the effort to see her and reconnect with her. My sobs grew stronger, the weight of remorse intensifying, yet her presence breathed new life into my soul.

The afternoon unfolded in a joyful family gathering, filled with the aroma of delicious *mole*, the warmth of *mezcal*, and the irresistible indulgence of churros. We danced and sang to the lively rhythms of ranchera music that played throughout the afternoon, immersing ourselves in the shared joy and nostalgia. As my aunts and uncles regaled me with stories of my mother and me during our time in El Romance, I found myself captivated by the tales of our past. With every laugh that echoed, every memory that resurfaced, and every story that was shared, I felt a growing reconnection with these people, both familiar and previously unknown. They became living vessels of our shared history, the keepers of stories long forgotten. In the embrace of their words, I felt a part of me that had lain dormant coming back to life. The tales woven around the gathering not only painted a vivid picture of my family's experiences, but they also reignited a flame within me. Memories that had slipped through the cracks of time found their way back into my consciousness, reclaiming their place in my heart. It was as if a dormant flame had been rekindled, illuminating the depths of my being with renewed vigor.

***

As the days turned into weeks and months in El Romance, I found myself extending my stay in México. There was nothing pulling me back to Los Angeles. Unwinding from the fast-paced life had its challenges. My internal alarm clock still woke me up at five o'clock in the morning, and in those initial months, I would jolt out of bed, gasping for air, thinking I needed to rush to the office. But as the realization settled in that it was no longer a part of my life, I would sit on the bed, unable to sleep, unsure of what to do with myself. The remainder of my student loan debt, which I had not finished paying and opted for deferring before leaving for México, haunted me relentlessly. The anxiety attacks would sneak up on me, tempting me to hop on a plane, return to Los Angeles, and dive back into the world of work and money-making. But the thought of going back to my previous life made me physically ill. Although I was physically in a different place, my body and mind had been conditioned for years to feel a sense of scarcity if I wasn't constantly working or advancing in my career and in life. I wondered when I would reach a point where I would feel satisfied with the amount of money, freedom, and balance in my life. How much was enough to make me truly happy? These questions lingered in my mind as I continued my journey of introspection in El Romance. I knew that finding contentment would require unraveling the deep-seated beliefs and conditioning that had shaped my perspective on success and fulfillment. It was a process that required confronting my fears, redefining my values, and challenging societal expectations.

Over time, I discovered solace in activities like reading, writing, visiting Mamá Juanita and reading to her, and going for walks. These simple acts brought a sense of healing and tranquility. Occasionally, I allowed myself the luxury of an afternoon nap. However, even in those moments of rest, anxiety would sometimes seize me, and I would feel guilt for not being productive. I had embraced a simple and sustainable lifestyle. I had moved into a modest studio, opting for a month-to-month rental arrangement. In the mornings, I savored meals prepared with organic ingredients at el Mercado. I found myself spending my afternoons visiting Mamá Juanita and listening to her stories. I rejoiced hearing her voice. The need to buy new clothes had vanished, and I spent my days comfortably dressed in jeans, a colorful huipil, and huaraches. I reflected on the countless times I had mindlessly purchased clothes that ended up forgotten in a closet for months or even years. Consumerism, once a driving force in my life, had lost its grip on me. The absence of materialistic pursuits allowed me to feel more authentic, healthier, and liberated. I relished in the freedom to take leisurely walks, grab coffee with the few friends I had made, or enjoy moments of solitude. The main plaza became a place of solace, where I could sit and contemplate life, immerse myself in a good book, or pour my thoughts into my journal. In this new reality, stress and anxiety slowly dissipated, replaced by a sense of peace and clarity. I had the mental space to delve into deep introspection and question the path I had taken. For so long, I had believed that becoming a lawyer and having a well-paying job would bring me happiness, but it hadn't. I began to ponder whether marriage and having children were the missing pieces that would complete my happiness. Observing my married cousins, who seemed content as housewives and mothers, stirred these thoughts within me. Leonardo's memory also resurfaced, prompting me to wonder if marrying him would have brought me the fulfillment I longed for. Though I had dated somewhat, I had not found a connection with any man like the one I had with Leonardo. I spent countless hours lost in reflection, contemplating my uncertain future and searching for my true purpose in life.

CHAPTER 16

Emilio

I WAS AWAKENED BY THE LIVELY FESTIVITIES OF MEXICAN Independence Day. The melodic tolling of the church bells announced the eight o'clock Mass. Intrigued by the joyous sounds of children's laughter, I looked out the balcony to catch a glimpse of them rushing to school in their flawless uniforms. Living near an elementary school, I could hear the marching band readying itself to play the Mexican national anthem. The flag ceremony, a customary tradition on such mornings, was about to commence. Eagerly, I positioned myself on the balcony, hoping to witness the entire event. Memories flooded my mind as I recalled my own school days in México, wearing a plaid skirt uniform, long white socks that reached my knees, and shiny, black patent leather shoes. I too had taken part in similar flag ceremonies, where we honored the Mexican flag and sang the national anthem. The student with the highest grade point average in the school had the privilege of carrying the Mexican flag across the playground, accompanied by a group of drummers marching in perfect unison. As the familiar strains of the national anthem began to play, a wave of nostalgia washed over me. Moved by the sentiment, I rose from my seat, placed my right hand over my chest in salute, and joined in singing along:

> Mexicanos, al grito de Guerra,
> El acero aprestad y el bridón,

Y retiemble en sus centros la tierra.
Al sonoro rugir del cañón

The resounding notes echoed along the cobblestone streets and seeped through the walls of my small studio. As the anthem finalized, I hurriedly dressed in a colorful *huipil* and *huaraches* and left my studio earlier than usual, driven by the anticipation of witnessing and immersing myself in the town's vibrant festivities. I made my way to my customary café, eager to see the town come alive in anticipation of the day's celebrations. I ordered a steaming café de olla and settled at a table that offered a picturesque view of the bustling plaza. The city had transformed itself into a radiant tapestry of green, white, and red, adorned with Mexican flags, ribbons, and flowers. A myriad of decorations adorned homes, balconies, and government buildings. As I sat there, I reveled in the colonial beauty of my town, basking in the richness of its culture. The crisp September morning added a touch of freshness and clarity to the scene, enhancing the sheer beauty of the moment. I found solace in the simplicity of it all, captivated by the elegance that surrounded me.

As I savored my café de olla, lost in a wave of nostalgia, I became aware of a presence from the corner of my eye. A tall, handsome man with a nerdy charm caught my attention, prompting me to observe him intently. There was an intriguing quality about him that I couldn't quite put into words. Suddenly, our eyes met, and he offered a friendly wave. Overwhelmed by a rush of teenage-like nervousness and embarrassment, I quickly averted my gaze, pretending to be engrossed in the pages of my book to avoid any further awkwardness. To my surprise, he seemed to perceive my unease and responded with a warm smile as he continued on his way across the bustling plaza. It was evident that he was a local, distinguishable from the typical tourists by his modest attire: no flashy clothing or ostentatious jewelry. Clad in a simple ensemble of jeans, work boots, a blue and white plaid shirt, and a hat, he exuded an air of authenticity. Unable to resist, I found myself following him with my gaze as he disappeared into the Municipal Palace building. Brushing aside any notions of a potential encounter, I refocused my attention on my book and the comforting presence of my café de olla.

I had just finished reading a couple of chapters when the waiter interrupted my solitude, placing a second cup of café de olla before me. Perplexed, I informed him that I hadn't ordered another coffee. With a knowing smile, the waiter replied, "It's from the young man at that table." He pointed to my right, where the nerdy-looking gentleman was looking back at me, respectfully bowing his head. A blush crept onto my cheeks, and I reciprocated with a smile, offering a slight bow of gratitude in return.

He approached my table and politely inquired, "Good morning, miss. I hope I'm not intruding, and please don't take it as a lack of respect for me to buy you coffee."

I was startled by the unexpected attention, it had been months since I had last flirted with someone. I was momentarily unsure of how to react. There was something about this man that stirred a tremor within me, akin to a leaf on the verge of falling from a tree. Gathering my composure, I replied, "Good morning. No, quite the opposite. Thank you. It's my favorite coffee."

A sense of relief washed over him as he introduced himself, saying, "Emilio. Nice to meet you." He extended his hand, and I rose from my seat to reciprocate the introduction.

"Lucia. The pleasure is mine."

"Lucia, would you mind if I join you?" Emilio asked.

"Of course not. Please, have a seat."

Although I had always been cautious about engaging with strangers, Emilio's presence sparked a sense of curiosity within me. Allowing my guard to lower, I welcomed him to join me at the table. As we conversed, our discussion ventured beyond the realms of the book I had been reading. We delved into life, our town, and the ongoing festivities. Emilio shared that he was a mathematics professor at a university in a city near El Romance. His parents, born in the city, had relocated to El Romance after marrying to pursue a better quality of life for him and his siblings. His father was a doctor, and his mother an elementary school teacher. Hearing about their academic achievements left me somewhat intimidated, as my own parents had not progressed beyond elementary school—an unspoken reminder of my humble upbringing. However, any concerns about our compatibility faded into insignificance as I listened to him speak. His intellect and charm were captivating. I found myself drawn to his light brown eyes and his neatly trimmed beard, lending him an essence of maturity. His lips were full, and each time he laughed, a charming dimple graced the left side of his cheek. His smile was gentle, and it revealed a flawless set of white teeth. His laughter was infectious, and in no time, I found myself yearning to unravel more about this man and spend additional moments in his company.

Emilio extended an invitation for me to join him at El Grito, the Mexican independence ceremony and celebration, that evening. Despite my attempts to temper my excitement, I'm sure my demeanor resembled that of a child receiving a long-awaited toy. It was the first time I spent Mexican independence day in México since I was a child and I was eager to partake in the ceremony. In addition, of course, I wanted to spend more time with Emilio. Hence, eagerly accepted the invitation and willingly allowed him to enter my uncertain life. From that crisp September morning onward, Emilio and I grew closer, our bond deepening with each passing day. He possessed a unique combination of intelligence, ambition, and chivalry, which swept me off my feet in a way no one had ever done in my adult life. In addition to taking me on enchanting horseback rides through the local mountains, he introduced me to numerous places beyond El Romance that I had never before experienced. We indulged in long picnics and engaged in profound conversations infused with effortless laughter by a nearby creek. There was an unmistakable sense that our meeting and subsequent connection were destined. It was as if a divine force had orchestrated our union.

Within just three months of our initial encounter, I was deeply in love with this man. He stood apart from all the others I had dated in the past. I cherished his fearlessness in loving me, his unwavering pursuit, and his clarity in expressing his intentions. With Emilio, there were no worries about whether he liked me, who would text first or of being ghosted. Everything unfolded organically and effortlessly.

***

On New Year's Eve, we joined his extended family at his grandfather's ranch for a celebration. As the clock struck midnight, Emilio went down on one knee and surprised me with an unexpected proposal. I was shocked and elated. The idea seemed impulsive or even crazy, but in my heart, it felt undeniably right. I recalled how cliché it had sounded when my married friends spoke of "knowing" when they found the one. Yet, with Emilio, that cliché transformed into my own reality—I simply knew he was the one and I joyfully accepted to marry him.

My decision to move back to the States in the new year was completely overturned by my engagement to Emilio. When I broke the news to my family, it triggered a wave of shock and disbelief. My mother's reaction bordered on a heart attack, and my father was deeply disappointed, struggling to comprehend my seemingly impulsive choice. He had uprooted our lives years ago, bringing me to the States to provide better opportunities, and now I was willingly leaving behind my hard-earned career and everything I had worked for, all for a man. It was difficult for them to grasp the significance of my decision and its suddenness. However, knowing my resolute nature, they eventually stopped questioning me. They reluctantly agreed to fly to México to meet Emilio. We arranged a dinner for our parents to meet, selecting one of El Romance's most enchanting restaurants for the occasion. My parents approached the meeting with trepidation, feeling self-conscious about their lack of formal education compared to Emilio's parents, who were professionals. They struggled to overcome the belief that one's socioeconomic status determined their worth as individuals. It took a considerable amount of effort on my part to help them feel at ease. Thankfully, the dinner turned out to be a success, and both sets of parents got along remarkably well. Emilio's parents adored me, while my parents were highly impressed by Emilio. They were particularly delighted to discover that he was born in El Romance and shared our religious beliefs and moral values. Although it was undoubtedly challenging for my parents to leave me behind, they ultimately gave me their blessing and entrusted Emilio with my heart and hand in marriage.

Emilio and I made the decision to move in together before tying the knot, despite my mother's reluctance due to her devout Catholic beliefs. She had hoped for me to live on my own until the wedding day. However, I had long shed the Catholic guilt ingrained in me during my upbringing. Our love was pure and genuine, and we believed that there was nothing sinful about living as a couple in the months leading up to our wedding. In fact, those months turned out to be some of the most beautiful and cherished moments of my life. Emilio made it a point to show me his deep affection and love, and I reciprocated by making him feel cherished and valued. We strolled through the town hand in hand, and Emilio proudly introduced me to his friends. I accompanied him to conferences, where I was always in awe of his eloquence and professionalism. There existed a profound admiration between us, not only on a personal level but also on a professional one. Our love was a love I had secretly dreamt of finding. In the weeks leading to our wedding, we were required to attend Mass on Sundays for several weeks as part of our wedding's religious ceremony. Despite no longer practicing my faith, I found myself trying to reignite it. Kneeling before the enormous crucifix hanging from the main altar, I thanked Him for sending Emilio into my life. He made me feel loved—more loved than I had ever felt.

***

Our wedding day arrived. I felt I had finally achieved success. It felt like I had finally found that missing piece to feeling fulfilled. Seeing myself in the mirror, I saw a beautiful and happy young woman. My stunning off-white satin dress that cascaded down to the floor felt like a pair of wings. My veil, which trailed below my waist, sparkled with crystal-like embellishments. My hair curled and flowed freely down my back. I reminisced about the days when as a little girl I twirled in Mamá Juanita's garden imagining I was a bride. My dream was now a reality.

The garden where we exchanged our vows, adorned with vibrant flowers and majestic jacaranda trees, served as a reminder of the beauty and magic of that day. The reception was larger than we had anticipated, with extended families on both sides in attendance. The presence of my closest friends, who had traveled from the States to be with us, added to the warmth and love surrounding us. It was a night filled with pure celebration, as we danced to the lively tunes of banda, indulged in mezcal, and rejoiced in our union. I danced and laughed with joy throughout the night. Amidst the festivities, I stole a moment to step away and gaze up at the clear sky. Gratitude overflowed from my heart. Finally, I felt a deep sense of happiness, as if living in a fairy tale.

After our enchanting wedding, Emilio and I embarked on our journey as a married couple. Our young love carried us through the early days of our marriage, as our relationship continued to blossom. As weeks turned into months, I found myself primarily tending to my husband's needs and staying home. Although I had never imagined myself as a housewife, I enjoyed the role.

***

As the months progressed, the desire to work and my passion for independence overtook me. I secured a temporary job as a paralegal at a law firm in the city where Emilio worked. The compensation I received for full-time work was dishearteningly low. The significant disparity between the workload and pay eventually left me disillusioned. In an attempt to further my legal career in México, I pursued a law degree. However, I became increasingly frustrated and discouraged by the complexities of the Mexican bureaucracy. I was disappointed by my inability to fully transfer my legal knowledge and skills to the Mexican legal system. As time took its course, I couldn't help but feel worried about my professional future. Despite Emilio's support, the fact that I had been out of work for over a year was unsettling. I missed the sense of fulfillment that came with earning my own money and using my legal skills. Although I tried to keep busy with reading, volunteering, cleaning the house, walking to the Mercado to buy groceries, visiting Mamá Juanita, and going on walks, I couldn't shake the worry that I began to feel.

Eventually, I managed to secure a position as an English professor at Emilio's university. I was thrilled at the opportunity to work alongside him and spend more time together. Just as things seemed to be falling into place, however, budget cuts hit, and English courses were removed from the curriculum. Once again, I found myself without a job and facing uncertainty. Months went by, and despite my efforts to find another teaching position, nothing materialized. I began to question whether I was truly happy or if I had allowed my love for Emilio to blind me to my own desires and aspirations. I missed the financial independence I had once enjoyed. I couldn't help but feel a sense of remorse for not being able to help my parents financially and for potentially losing the legal skills I had worked so hard to develop. To make matters worse, Emilio's focus shifted entirely to his career. He became consumed by his desire for a prestigious role at the university and his political ambitions. He worked until late and travel frequently. The nights spent alone became unbearable, and I resented how his goals took precedence over our relationship.

Communication became strained. I began to notice brief sparks of anger that ignited within him when I expressed feeling neglected, but I disregarded them, believing that no one is perfect. Yet, it was difficult to reconcile the man I fell in love with, who pursued me with passion and charm, with the person he had become. To keep the peace, I opted to keep my emotions to myself, shutting down in my unhealthy thoughts. Yet, a hurricane of emotions was forming, resentment was brewing, and erosion of our connection and our happiness was gradually taking force.

Two years into our marriage, it was evident that we had lost sight of our true selves amidst the pressures of our own fears and egos. Emilio's pursuit of success and external validation had taken a toll on our relationship. His focus on professional achievements overshadowed our connection. Meanwhile, my own fears about sacrificing my career and becoming a housewife consumed me. I had worked hard to establish myself as a professional, and the thought of completely giving up my independence and financial stability weighed heavily on my mind. I didn't want to rely solely on Emilio for financial support, and I feared losing my sense of self-worth that came from my career accomplishments. In this struggle, our egos clashed. Emilio's ambition fueled his drive for success, while my fears pushed me to hold onto my professional identity. We both became so fixated on these external factors that we lost sight of the true meaning of our relationship and the importance of supporting and understanding each other's dreams. We became distant and unable to express our true feelings and concerns. Instead of finding a middle ground and working together to address our individual needs, we allowed our fears and desires to drive us further apart. Eventually, I couldn't help but question whether love alone was enough to sustain us. The road ahead felt uncertain, and I wondered if we would ever find our way back to each other, or if the decay had taken hold and would consume us completely.

I kept my struggles hidden from friends and family, believing that vulnerability was a weakness and that I needed to handle everything on my own. I didn't want to burden my loved ones with my worries and concerns. After all, I had always been strong and resilient in overcoming challenges in the past. I believed I could overcome this one too. From the outside, we appeared to be the epitome of a happy and accomplished couple. People saw us as a symbol of love that could beat all odds – the love story of a lawyer and a professor brought together by El Romance. But behind closed doors, we had allowed our insecurities and fears to erode the foundation of our marriage. As time went on, the deterioration of our relationship became evident. Our once-deep connection was distant. The love we felt for each other was buried beneath layers of doubt and fear. It was a painful realization to see how we had allowed our marriage to be shaped by external factors and the demands of our egos. We had unintentionally allowed our union to crumble. We had a choice to make: to continue down this path of decay or to reevaluate our priorities, reconnect with our core values, and rebuild our marriage on a foundation of love and mutual support. It wasn't easy, but I was willing to confront my fears and face our vulnerabilities together.

***

The week prior to my thirty-sixth birthday, Emilio had been away for work. I had made arrangements to celebrate with our friends upon his return. He had assured me that he would be back from his trip on the evening of my celebration, but he would meet me at the restaurant before our friends arrived. The day had been chaotic, but I eagerly anticipated reuniting with my husband after a long week and rejoicing with him. I purchased a special dress, hoping to appear exceptionally beautiful. I yearned to captivate my husband, just as I had on the day we first met at the plaza. My deepest desire was to reignite our mutual admiration. I arrived at the restaurant before any of our guests and promptly called Emilio to inform him of my presence. However, he did not answer. Throughout the entire week, he had been unresponsive to my texts and calls, causing several arguments between us. Nonetheless, I firmly believed that night would be an opportunity to make up. As an hour ticked by without a word from Emilio, my first guests arrived. I began to celebrate with them, but the nagging notion that something might have happened to Emilio persisted in my mind. Paradoxically, I found myself secretly hoping for one of his customary excuses—those "I couldn't answer the phone" explanations he often used—rather than the possibility of something happening to him. I sent him several texts, yet received no response. By the time all of our guests had arrived, I instinctively knew that something was amiss.

Two hours had passed since Emilio was expected to arrive when suddenly my phone rang—it was an unknown number. I experienced a mix of relief and anger.

"Hi Lucia, its Soraya, Emilio's new assistant. He asked me to call you and inform you that he is not going to make it."

"New assistant? He has not mentioned you. Why couldn't he call me?"

"I'm not sure why, but he was invited to a last minute dinner with the university director and some politicians. He told me to emphasize the significance of this event for his career. He said he would call you later."

As I quietly listened to the woman speak, my heart sank. I was so furious that I felt no relief to confirm he was okay. Maintaining my composure, I hung up without saying anything further. I was at a loss as to how to make him comprehend the impact of his decisions on our relationship. Despite my efforts to express my feelings of neglect, he remained unresponsive. He justified his behavior by claiming that everything he did was for our benefit.

In that moment, I grappled with a flood of emotions—anger, sadness, and disappointment. I had attempted to be supportive of Emilio's dreams and aspirations, but it began to feel like a contradiction. Was I sacrificing my own happiness to uphold my husband's ambitions?

After ending the call in silence, I took a moment to regain my composure before returning to meet my guests, wearing a forced smile. I shared the disappointing news that Emilio wouldn't be able to join us due to an urgent work matter. Drawing upon my strength, I portrayed an optimistic demeanor, attempting to laugh and celebrate with my friends. Deep down, however, I concealed a simmering mix of disappointment, anger, resentment, and sadness that had been steadily accumulating within me over the past year. My fairy tale had strayed far from the path of a blissful "happily ever after."

***

In the months that followed, I immersed myself in the struggle of trying to salvage my marriage, enduring personal sacrifices and suppressing my own emotions. I had implored Emilio to attend couple's therapy, but he adamantly refused, claiming he was too busy. Consequently, I began therapy sessions for myself. My therapist emphasized that I could only heal and work on my own part, unable to change or force Emilio to do the same. Marriage required the effort of both individuals, and I couldn't be the sole bearer of communication, compromise, and sacrifice. Despite having sacrificed so much for the sake of our marriage, I felt abandoned in return. My thoughts turned to my mother, who had endured years of emotional neglect to preserve her marriage and provide a stable home for her children. My father dedicated his life to having two jobs while she had dedicated herself to supporting my father and raising us, relinquishing her own dreams. I also thought of Mamá Juanita, who had been forced to marry and suffered greatly in her marriage to Papá Lucho. I grappled with conflicting emotions, torn between guilt for wanting to end my marriage and accepting the notion that enduring unhappiness was necessary to save it. I was taught to sacrifice my own dreams and desires to salvage my marriage.

Being in México over two years, I had become aware of my extended family's gossip and drama and it was evident that the majority of women in my family had endured infidelity, neglect, physical, emotional, and sexual abuse within their marriages. Their unions had only endured for years at the expense of their own happiness. I resisted the cycle perpetuated by my culture and religion, following in the footsteps of my mother, grandmother and the married females in my family. I had heard my *tías* speak of their marriages as their *cruz* or cross to bear—a choice they made, carrying its weight until death, similar to Jesus Christ's crucifixion. However, something about this concept didn't sit right with me.

I resisted becoming another woman trapped in an unhappy marriage, taking pride in enduring misery for decades. I faced a difficult decision: either follow the path of sacrifice like my mother and grandmother, maintaining the bond of marriage, or break the cycle and subject myself to society's harsh judgment. I could clearly hear the criticisms of the women in my family, cousins and aunts chastising me for breaking the sanctity of marriage. No woman in my lineage had ever divorced. Could I be the first woman in my family to do so? Could I bear my own mother's disapproval? I spent months in turmoil.

When I finally mustered the courage to tell Emilio that our relationship could not continue as it was, he responded by prioritizing his dreams and career. I was deeply hurt, and my defense mechanism prompted me to remind him of the many sacrifices I had made for our union, including leaving my career as a lawyer, my family and life in the US. His cold response, though harsh, was true: he had never asked me to sacrifice anything for him; it was a choice I had willingly made. I had to confront the reality that I alone could not continue sacrificing everything. I alone could not save the relationship. Resentment was poisoning me, and I was unable to carry that burden any longer. Yet, the thought of boarding a plane back to Los Angeles and facing my family and society after a failed marriage was terrifying. If I returned to Los Angeles after leaving Emilio, I had to face the consequences of a broken heart while simultaneously enduring society's judgment for my marital failure. Could I sacrifice everything—my happiness, career, financial independence, and all that I had tirelessly worked for—to save my marriage? I was utterly torn.

CHAPTER 17

Surrender

I COULD HEAR THE RAIN GRADUALLY DISSIPATING, ITS GENTLE sound fading away. The open window allowed the cold morning breeze to sneak into my bedroom, caressing my back with an icy touch that made me shiver, forcing me to reluctantly change positions. A faint fragrance of dried eucalyptus leaves, decaying in a vase next to my bed, served as a reminder that I was still alive. The birds were chirping joyfully, and the sun was slowly ascending the horizon, compelling the clouds and rain to conclude their performance. As I slowly emerged from the depths of slumber, the dampness on my pillow persisted, evidence of another night spent in tears. Opening my eyes, I immediately felt the weight of existence pressing upon me once again. I lay motionless in bed, listening as the sounds of the urban morning gradually overpowering the birds' melodious songs.

The morning light snuck in through the chinks and looked at me with pity. I shifted to my back with the little energy I had left in my body. As I looked toward the ceiling, a light tear escaped my right eye and rolled down my cheek before landing on the pillow. I was tired of crying. I turned to the right and rolled my body into the fetal position, wishing never to leave my bed. I had turned off my alarm, but it didn't matter; I had been unable to sleep most of the night. A sense of hopelessness washed over me, accompanied by a feeling of brokenness, fear, guilt, and an overwhelming sense of isolation. My loss consumed me entirely, rendering everything else in life seemingly insignificant. A surge of anger and resentment coursed through me, fueled by the weight of being alive. I couldn't help but entertain the thoughts of self-blame. Perhaps if I hadn't consumed the salmon salad the day before, the cramps wouldn't have started. Maybe if I had taken better care of my body, shed the excess weight that had been advised, this tragedy could have been averted. What if I hadn't subjected my body to immense stress following my separation from Emilio? Would my baby still be nestled within my womb? Could it be that my age, and the prioritization of my career over starting a family, had played a part in this heart-wrenching situation? The echoes of societal expectations haunted me, reminding me of the warnings I received throughout my teenage years and early adulthood: the dire consequences of getting pregnant outside of wedlock, a sin of great magnitude.

Consequently, my fear of pregnancy became a constant companion during my twenties, leading me to endure the shame and fear associated with sexual activity outside of marriage, as well as the stress of pursuing methods of contraception when I became sexually active. Ironically, when I graduated from law school and dedicated myself to my career, the narrative changed. The question shifted to "When will you have a child?" but the underlying tone remained one of reproach: "You're getting older; if you don't act soon, you may lose the opportunity to conceive, Lucia." These messages, delivered by extended family, acquaintances, friends, and society as a whole, had insidiously infiltrated my consciousness, causing me to shoulder years of unwarranted stress. Each thought bombarded me, and I held myself accountable for internalizing and believing this rhetoric and subjecting my body to the relentless strain it brought. Immobilized in my bed, I felt a sense of revulsion toward a society that persistently dictated how women should feel about their bodies, their sexuality, and their decisions surrounding motherhood. Was I facing punishment for daring to challenge these expectations?

As I ruminated on my circumstances, my thoughts turned to Emilio, and I directed blame toward him. He was completely unaware of what was unfolding. During our last argument, he reached his boiling point, and he walked out of our home, declaring that he was done with our marriage. In a matter of hours, he packed his belongings and vanished from my life. Weeks had passed without a word from him, and he remained oblivious to my pregnancy. I had deliberately chosen not to inform him, as I refused to become the kind of woman who uses a child as a means to cling to a man or maintain a failing marriage. Deep in my heart, I knew our relationship was beyond repair, and I didn't want to prolong our misery by attempting to stay together for the sake of our child. I had made the decision to disclose my pregnancy to Emilio when I reached the second trimester. The first trimester had been a tumultuous battle, both physically and emotionally. During that time, I was grieving the demise of our marriage while simultaneously grappling with the overwhelming happiness that pregnancy had bestowed upon me. These two opposing emotions waged war within me, leaving me trapped in a constant cycle of tearful sorrow and tearful joy.

In moments of disbelief, I still found it hard to accept that my marriage had crumbled. However, in comparison, the pain of losing my child overshadowed everything else. It shattered me completely. Letting Emilio go was difficult, but acknowledging the loss of my child was an unimaginable reality to confront. I replayed that day in my mind countless times, desperately searching for where I had gone wrong. I had recently been hired by a law firm in Los Angeles. I had just finished defending a deposition when I first felt the onset of intense cramps in my abdomen and back. The pain grew increasingly severe as the day progressed. When I went to the restroom, a surge of panic washed over me as I noticed bright red blood in the toilet. My heart stopped beating for several agonizing seconds. I immediately rushed myself to the hospital, gripped by a sense of dread.

Flashes of the doctor's poker face expression during the blood tests and ultrasound haunted my mind incessantly. I remained in the hospital gown, lying on the frigid bed, waiting for results. When he finally entered the room, he had a somber countenance. His broad forehead and sunken eyes surrounded by dark circles, his face almost skeletal in appearance, communicated the news even before he uttered a word. Seating himself on the stool beside me, he locked his gaze with mine and delivered the devastating message. "It appears that you have experienced a miscarriage." It took several seconds for the weight of his words to register in my mind. Tears streamed down my face as the reality sank in. Denial washed over me, and I shook my head, desperately attempting to conceal the overwhelming emotions that surged through my body. My heart sank, consumed by a pain unlike anything I had ever experienced before. The doctor continued, "Based on the testing and your symptoms, it seems that this pregnancy was abnormal. The fetus was not viable, and even if it had survived, the baby would have faced severe congenital issues. This was the best outcome."

I couldn't fathom how the doctor could suggest that this tragedy was for the best. How could God allow such a devastating event to unfold? The pregnancy had been the sole remaining connection to the beauty of my love with Emilio, and now it had been utterly extinguished. With great difficulty, I managed to gather myself and return home, carrying the weight of my lifeless body. In the days that ensued, my world crumbled around me. I was enveloped in an impenetrable darkness, consumed by inconsolable sobs that wracked my body. I surrendered myself to the overwhelming anguish of my shattered heart, lying in bed devoid of any motivation to continue living or moving forward. Curled up beneath the comforting embrace of a plush white blanket, a witness to my sleepless nights and the repository of countless tears, I found myself at the lowest point of my existence. Time seemed to drag on, with each hour passing with a sense of uncertainty hanging in the air. There were moments when the temptation to surrender to the desire to end my life seemed alluring. The thought of escaping this world and its immense suffering held an inexplicable appeal. There were times when succumbing to the pain seemed easier, as the tears that flowed from my eyes like an endless river, briefly carried away the weight of my anguish. Not eating and not sleeping became preferable to the arduous task of carrying on. The absence of sleep was more bearable than enduring nightmares that inflicted the pain upon me once again. Despair and emptiness infiltrated every cell of my being, while the isolation of my suffering left me without anyone to share my pain with.

In the midst of overwhelming pain, I reached a breaking point where the weight in my heart became too much to bear. My spirit was crushed, and I couldn't fathom how I would ever emerge from the deep, dark hole I had fallen into. In fact, a part of me didn't even desire to climb out. I longed to be swallowed by the confines of that desolate pit and disappear forever. In that moment, I slowly rose from the bed, pulling my bare legs out from beneath the comforting warmth of the blankets that had been my refuge for days. As my toes touched the cold, wooden floor, a shiver ran up my legs and spine, a reminder of the stark reality that surrounded me. My gaze landed upon the nightstand, where two unopened bottles of Zoloft and Xanax beckoned me, their contents holding the allure of an escape. With hesitation, I stood up and reached for the bottles, my trembling hands reflecting the turmoil within. Opening the bottles, I emptied the blue and white pills into the palm of my hand. As I brought the pills closer to my mouth, my sobs intensified. Choking on my own tears, I collapsed to my knees. Some of the pills slipped from my grasp, scattering across the floor. With the remaining pills in my hand, a moment of desperation gripped me. The weight of my sorrow seemed insurmountable, and in that haze of pain, I didn't stop to consider the consequences. I consumed the pills, ready to surrender to the darkness that enveloped me. My body convulsed with sobs and I gasped for a breath between desperate cries.

The last thing I remembered was that as I lay on the floor, my body drained of strength and my spirit engulfed in turmoil, my gaze fixated on the wall across from the bed where a picture of Mamá Juanita hung next to a crucifix. Her gentle smile radiated pure joy, and her long, white hair cascaded delicately over her fragile shoulders. There was an undeniable aura of peace and tranquility that washed over her. It was as though her gaze was fixed upon me, filled with a love so tender and comforting that it embraced my entire being. Her usual words, "Ponte en las manos de Dios," came to my mind—then, a surge of embarrassment flooded over me. Raising my quivering right arm toward her picture, I yearned to transcend the confines of my current existence. I turned my gaze to the agonized face of Jesus on the crucifix next to Mamá Juanita's picture. Stripped of everything, wearing only a crown of thorns and a thin cloth covering his pelvis, he bore the weight of unbearable pain. His features contorted in anguish, blood streaming from his forehead, hands, and feet, pierced by merciless nails. A parallel emerged in my mind—Jesus, too, had been abandoned by God in his final moments on the cross. In that moment of utter despair, with nothing left to lose, I lacked the desire to offer a prayer for any specific request. Yet, the words found their way from my lips, escaping into the stillness of the room: "I do not know if you really exist. I haven't talked to you in a long time. All I know is that I feel abandoned too. I can't anymore. I surrender."

With the image of my grandmother's joyful smile imprinted in my mind, and the warmth of her smile enveloping me, I embraced the notion of surrender and relinquishing control. I felt as if an unseen force took hold of my being, guiding my actions and thoughts. A fragile glimmer of hope flickered within me, a silent acknowledgment that perhaps there was something beyond my comprehension, something that could provide solace in the depths of my anguish. Exhausted, I lay on the cold floor, my body and soul intertwined as I felt a divine embrace where I found solace and extreme peace. I then lost consciousness.

CHAPTER 18

Seeds

I STOOD ON A BALCONY, OVERLOOKING ONE OF THE MANY RED stone mountains composed of asymmetric monoliths that rose above a blanket of green pines. The sun had already set, and as the town embraced darkness with minimal artificial lighting, the stars began to appear brighter. The color of the mountains intensified with the setting sun. I closed my eyes and took a deep breath, feeling the warm breeze gently caress my face. It felt as if the journey leading up to this day had been long and arduous, leaving me physically and emotionally exhausted. In the distance, I heard the soft whisper of a creek. Eager to reach the water, I allowed the sound of it to guide me. Within minutes, I arrived at the creek's edge, greeted by a grassy area by the bank. Without hesitation, I rested on the grass, facing upwards, stretching my legs and arms outward. I surrendered to the enveloping night. Gazing at the sky, I watched as more distant stars gradually emerged, one by one, like curious elves peeking out from behind trees in a lush forest. Countless stars adorned the heavens, each possessing its own beauty, but some shining brighter than others. I lay there immersing myself in the vast, twinkling expanse of the night sky. The fresh grass pricked through my white linen pants and cloak, gently reminding me of my connection to the earth, grounding me in the present moment.

An elderly woman with long white hair suddenly appeared from nowhere. She stood by my side and looked down on me.

Her presence radiated warmth. She extended her arm, gesturing for me to rise. Adorning her head was a beautiful clip made of black, white, and turquoise feathers, blending harmoniously with her white hair. Turquoise jewelry adorned her, including a necklace, earrings, and rings on each index finger. She was clad in a white tunic and leather huaraches. Her dusty feet and toenails peeked through the straps and her tanned skin exuded a sense of long travel by foot. Though I couldn't see her face, her comforting aura enveloped me. Her voice was soft and serene. Her wizard-like appearance provided reassurance, prompting me to trustingly extend my arm and allow her to help me to my feet. As she briefly held my hand, she signaled for me to follow her. We walked through the night in silence until we reached a mountaintop just as the first light of dawn began to grace the horizon. Several clouds were hanging in the sky. Red Rock Mountain stood majestically before me. The layers of different colors of rock started to change as the sun began to rise in the east behind a cluster of altocumulus clouds. Below us stretched a valley surrounded by majestic canyons of red rock. The sheer beauty of this place was awe-inspiring, as if it had been meticulously crafted by the hands of God. Taking a few deep breaths, I closed my eyes and embraced the serene beauty of the morning.

Breaking the silence, the woman asked, "Why are you here?" Her question caught me off guard. I was unsure of why I had arrived in that place. Startled, I looked at her with confusion, but she gently persisted, "Why are you here?" Collecting my thoughts, I attempted to articulate a thoughtful response. Sensing my deep contemplation, she reassured me, saying, "It's not a difficult question."

"I am lost," I blurted out, my words filled with a mix of desperation and longing. "I'm uncertain of what brought me here." I continued, "Something within me feels incomplete. I carry an immense burden of suffering and sadness. I am plagued by anger, fear, guilt, and resentment. The pain that consumes my heart has become unbearable. I lost my child. My marriage has crumbled, and I find no joy in my career or in life. I am exhausted from tirelessly pursuing my desires, only to be left empty and unfulfilled." The weight of my emotions overwhelmed me; tears streamed down my face uncontrollably.

"You have endured so much, but your experiences have shaped you into who you are today. You are exactly where you are meant to be. However, there are some lessons that you must learn. The first lesson you must learn is that every human being on Earth is on a unique journey. No two journeys are alike, and no journey lasts forever. Your child had its own individual journey, as did your ex-husband. They were part of your journey for a specific purpose, but once that purpose was fulfilled, they had to continue on their own paths, just as you must continue on yours. Neither you nor they could escape this reality.

"What did you learn from your experience of being pregnant?"

I wiped away the tears from my eyes, recalling the profound sense of vitality that surged through me when I first discovered I was carrying life within. In that moment, I felt chosen by a higher power; a profound pride and beauty enveloped me. I fell in love with a soul I had not yet met, free from fear or reservation. I felt alive, complete, and incredibly special like never before. It was difficult for me to comprehend how such a tragic loss, like losing my child, could possibly teach me anything. I remained silent, struggling to find the right words to express my thoughts.

"Go on," she encouraged me gently. "You have learned something. I know it."

Taking a deep breath, I began to speak, my words hesitant and restrained. "Well, for years, I had avoided pregnancy at all costs, believing that it could negatively affect my future and professional success. I had convinced myself that I couldn't get pregnant out of wedlock. Hence, when I found out I was pregnant, I embraced the experience of carrying life within me. I learned to love my body as I witnessed the miraculous growth of my belly, and it transformed my perception of myself. I experienced a profound connection and a sense of wonderment."

"And what did you learn after the loss?" she inquired further.

"The pain I endured was excruciating. It wasn't only the physical pain but also the emotional anguish that consumed me. That pain was far more intense. I was overwhelmed by guilt, a feeling of being undeserving, of shame, and remorse. It felt as if I had lost a part of myself. I directed my anger toward myself and my ex-husband. I blamed him, and I blamed myself too."

"But what did you learn?" she persisted.

I took a moment to reflect, my mind grappling with the lessons hidden within my experience. "I learned what it truly feels like to hit rock bottom," I replied.

She interrupted gently, "No. You learned to surrender. It was the first time you truly surrendered."

Surprised by her insight, I listened intently as she continued.

"Many believe that when you hit rock bottom there is no way out. However, there is a way. The way is up. Now, how you go up depends on you, you can either go up through struggle or you can go up through surrender. When you surrender, you do not give up, you let the Universe take the lead."

I struggled to understand her words, but remained captivated.

"Your worth as a woman is not dependent on becoming a mother. True happiness does not solely rely on motherhood. You are just as beautiful and worthy as any woman, regardless of whether you bear children or not. The societal pressure imposed on women to be mothers is unjust. You have no control over that. Obsessing over it only perpetuates the expectations and norms forced upon us by society, dictating what defines a 'real' woman and how we should be valued. Women who have children do so because their purpose intertwines with that of their child. Your purpose is different. Nothing external, beyond what resides within you, can replace the power you possess to fulfill your unique purpose. Beside, embodying the qualities of a mother does not require you to give birth to a child. You can love and nurture just as a biological mother can."

Her words resonated deeply within me. It was as if a part of my being had been waiting to hear and embrace these words. Up to that point, it had not crossed my mind that there were lessons in my painful experience.

"What about your marriage ending? What did that teach you?" she inquired.

This time, I was ready with an answer. The pain of Emilio's departure had haunted me for months. "I learned what it feels to be abandoned."

"Lucia, no one can abandon you but yourself. Emilio's decision to leave was not an abandonment of you, but rather a consequence of the dynamics and circumstances within your relationship. In the aftermath of his departure, you sank into a state of despair and self-blame and neglected to nurture and care for yourself. True abandonment occurs when we abandon ourselves, when we neglect our own happiness, and when we fail to recognize our own worth. It was your own neglect of your needs, your self-worth, and your well-being that left you feeling abandoned."

The wisdom in her words shook me.

"Besides, your identity as a woman does not hinge on having a man by your side. Did you not discover some beauty of finding peace by letting him go?"

"I did. After he left, I had peace. There was no more fighting. There was silence. I found strength within myself to carry on, even though some criticized my choice for divorce. I recognize that there was beauty in my courage to love someone deeply, risking that my heart might be broken, but still allowing myself to try."

"Emilio's purpose in your life was to lead you to a profound understanding of the incredible power you possess, regardless of the circumstances life throws at you," she stated. Her gaze locked with mine. "You harnessed the pain of your crisis to ignite that inner power within you. From now on, you will never seek strength in any external place or person because your strength lies solely within your own spirit."

As I absorbed her words, I realized that her guidance was urging me to let go. It was all about releasing the past and reflecting on the lessons I had learned from each experience. No matter how painful the situation, there was always a lesson to be gleaned. The woman looked at me with her deep, penetrating black eyes and spoke again. "You can now let go of it all. It's about embracing the art of letting go and asking yourself what you have learned from each circumstance. There is always a lesson, no matter how excruciating the situation may be.

"Follow me." Intrigued and filled with newfound hope, I decided to trust her and take the leap, following her lead into the unknown. As we ascended to the summit of the mountain, the woman continued to share her wisdom, intertwining her teachings with the knowledge of the land, and the native flora and fauna that surrounded us. With each step, I absorbed her words, eager to learn from her wisdom. She told me that 330 million years before, the entire valley was under water. Red Rock had been at the bottom of the ocean. The white rock above the red rock was above sea level and it was sand that was now solidified.

"The creator of this beauty had immense power to come up with something so extraordinary. That very same creator was your creator," she said. "You have been made by the same artist who created this landscape. You too are evolving into an extraordinary creation. Like the Red Rock Mountains, you have markings that time and life has left imprinted in your soul. Every scar, every fall, every challenge, every tear, every disappointment, every detour, every change of plans was meant to be part of your personal journey and has brought you to this very moment. Just like the mountain before you, you have slopes, valleys, inclines, steep embankments, and smooth terrain. You too are perfectly, imperfect." She convinced me.

She then guided me to a grove of wild cacti and agave plants, pointing out the majestic Agave Americana species that stood tall. She explained that these plants held great significance to my ancestors, who had utilized them for various purposes. From their hearts, they had extracted *agua miel*, the sap of the plant that has therapeutic qualities. When fermented, it is turned into *pulque*, a sacred beverage reserved for the gods and their priests. It eventually became a drink for the people, produced widely around the central Mexican highlands. The leaves were used for crafting essential household items, such as rugs and baskets. I marveled at the resilience of these plants, their sharp, succulent leaves glistening in the sunlight. They symbolized the strength and adaptability of my heritage, a reminder that I, too, possessed the power to endure and transform.

"Come closer. Look at this one. This one is about five years old. This is a female agave; you can tell because the leaves open clockwise. The male agave's leaves open counterclockwise. I want you to look at the leaves, *las pencas*. You see in the inside, the leaf has the imprint of the leaves that it nurtured, but on the outside, it has the imprints of those that nurtured it. You are like the agave. You are growing. You have nurtured others, and others have nurtured you. The imprints of your experiences are just like the imprints of the *pencas*." The woman encouraged me to connect with the agave plants, to touch their spiky leaves, and caress the smoothness of its *pencas*. The agave's life cycle mirrored the ebb and flow of my own existence. My experiences, although harsh, were necessary for my growth and evolution. In that moment, I understood that my journey was not only about personal healing but also about reconnecting with my roots, understanding where I came from, embracing the trials and tribulations of my ancestors, and honoring the lessons that my own experiences were providing for me.

"This one has reached its point of maturity. Its stem is out and filled with seeds. When the pockets open up, the wind and birds will carry its seeds across the land, those seeds will land on the earth and grow into new agaves and this agave will die as it will have completed its life's journey. All living things are born, go through rough situations or climates, some die in the process, others continue to grow and flourish, some reproduce, some don't, but all have a life cycle that they must complete. Everything and everyone in nature has its own journey. Something has sparked inside of you, and it will shoot up like the stem of this agave, and from within will come seeds that will spread, grow, and flourish."

I felt a sense of liberation as I embraced the understanding that I, too, had the potential to produce seeds of change and growth. Within me, something stirred, like the budding stem of the mature agave, ready to release its seeds into the world. It was a transformative moment as I realized that my own journey was not confined to suffering and loss but held the promise of new beginnings and flourishing.

"Now, close your eyes, take a deep breath, and hold it." I complied. "You are standing on a vortex of masculine energy. Masculine energy has been weighing heavily on you. Your child was a boy, and Emilio—well, both were masculine energies. You can now let go. Let them go, and let the pain attached to their memory go. You must remember: you do not need them or anyone else to complete your journey."

As I stood there, following the woman's instructions, with my eyes closed and breathing hard and long as she had instructed, I could sense a shift in the energy around me, a swirling of heavy energy that seemed to have held me captive for far too long and was tied to the memories of my child and Emilio. With her gentle guidance, the woman spoke words that penetrated deep into my soul. "Let go. Let them go," she urged me. "The burdens you carried, the longing and the pain, no longer serve a purpose in your journey," she whispered.

As the memories of Emilio and my lost child rested within my mind, I pretended to take them into the palms of my hands.

I visualized their weight, their hold on me. I could feel the significance of their presence, the pain they had caused, and the attachments that had kept me bound. I lifted my arms and opened my palms; a surge of determination and liberation coursed through me. With a deliberate intention, I let go. I released their memories, allowing them to be carried away by the gentle breeze that swept through the mountaintop. I opened my eyes and watched as two hummingbirds soared into the open sky, carried by the currents of freedom. They disappeared beyond the red rock mountains, merging with the vastness of the horizon. As they disappeared from sight, I felt a profound release within me. A sense of peace washed over me. The weight of their memories had lifted, leaving behind a newfound lightness of being. I embraced the beauty of the valley below, its vastness mirroring what I felt within. The woman stood beside me, her presence a testament to the wisdom and guidance she had bestowed upon me. She looked at me and I looked back, sharing a silent acknowledgment of the transformation that was taking place within me.

CHAPTER 19

True Love

As we made our way toward what she referred to as a second vortex named Heart Mountain, the increasing heat gradually erased the morning's crispness. Walking together in the northern part of the valley, the woman shared with me that her ancestors had resided in this area before migrating to central México. Furthermore, she mentioned that her inherited spirituality came from her mother. She proceeded to clarify that spirituality is not confined to any specific religion, but rather, it serves as a means to establish a connection with a higher power or who most know as God. This connection is deeply personal, allowing individuals the freedom to cultivate their own unique relationship with the higher power. She explained that each of us possesses access to this divine and healing energy and can learn to connect with it through various practices such as meditation, prayer, silent contemplation, and immersing oneself in nature.

By the time we reached the base of Heart Mountain, the clock neared noon. The trail stretched for miles amidst red rock formations and untamed cacti. Despite the heat, a peculiar sense of mental and physical readiness accompanied me through the captivating wilderness. With every step we took, the landscape grew increasingly lush and breathtaking. As we ventured farther along the crimson path, the enigmatic woman by my side continued probing me with questions about my life. As I walked and continued to learn and to unlearn lessons ingrained in my subconscious mind during my time with this woman, I found myself placing unwavering trust in her. Just as we began ascending uphill, she turned to me and in a soft voice said, "Tell me about your father."

"My father is a remarkable man. He possesses an exceptional work ethic and consistently held two jobs to ensure our well-being," I replied. Although I acknowledged that my father wasn't flawless, I believed he had never let me down. I couldn't help but wonder why she was specifically interested in him.

"You must have hardly seen him if he was juggling two jobs," she remarked.

"It is true," I admitted. "Before we relocated to the United States, he was rarely present. When I was born, he was already working abroad. It wasn't until I turned two that he returned. He stayed with us for a few months before returning to work in the US. His comings and goings, with him being away for extended periods, became a cycle. As I grew older, I yearned for his presence as he was always absent. Even when we moved to the United States, he remained incredibly busy, work consumed him and I rarely had the opportunity to spend time with him."

"Lucia, what you're describing is a deep-seated wound. Your father's hard work and sacrifice were driven by his love for you and your family, but as a child, you lacked the ability to comprehend that such sacrifices were expressions of love. For a child, love is understood through physical affection and quality time. Your father's inconsistent presence created mixed signals. When he was home, he may have shown you physical affection, but then he would leave for extended periods, leaving that affection absent. This kind of inconsistency can confuse a child and lead them to believe that a lack of constant affection is normal. Consequently, as an adult, you may seek partners who provide only fleeting moments of love and gratification."

Her words mirrored my own experiences. While Leonardo had shown me affection, his love was conditional, only embracing the parts of me that aligned with his beliefs and desires. The moment I aspired for personal growth and more from life, his support vanished. Similarly, Emilio had initially showered me with love but gradually became emotionally distant. Emilio loved me deeply but became so consumed by his career that he gradually disconnected from our relationship. I had allowed this to happen because the belief that such was true love had become ingrained in my subconscious mind.

"What's crucial for you to understand, Lucia, is that you are no longer that vulnerable child. You deserve to receive unconditional love and affection. However, it begins with loving and showing affection to yourself first. Cultivate a profound self-love that is so powerful that only those who can love you equally and genuinely are allowed into your life. As children, we become conditioned to the emotional energies that surround us, and our state of harmony and love is lost. We begin to feel insecure, afraid, and so many other emotions that do not correlate to our inherent nature of being at peace and in tune with love. This is not our fault, because we are unable to control who our parents and caregivers are and the environments we grow up in. However, it is our responsibility as adults to seek that state of harmony and love that becomes lost within the trauma that we accumulate as we become adults. As adults, we have the power to heal and to become aware of the unhealthy energies and behaviors that we learned from our caregivers and environments. We can learn to put an end to the unhealthy cycles we learned as children so that we do not repeat them. Most of us carry the weight of our generational trauma, and while breaking the cycle is never easy, it is our duty to liberate ourselves from it. Lucia, your inner child suffered wounds that left you feeling unloved, and that longing for love has driven you to chase it throughout your life. You craved that feeling of being loved, so you chose partners who initially offered just enough love to draw you in, but ultimately were unable to truly love you. As a result, the relationships ended, leaving you feeling unloved, unworthy, and utterly disappointed—much like the emotions you experienced every time your father had to leave."

The woman's words prompted me to reflect on the countless things I had tolerated from Emilio and other men I had dated, things that were far from being expressions of love. I had tolerated disrespect, neglect, lies, and even infidelity. I recalled how Emilio would react with anger whenever I requested more quality time or physical affection, as if my simple needs were personal attacks and accusations of his inadequacy as a partner. These situations left me feeling sad, disappointed, and upset. Yet, I often found myself justifying them, making excuses, or believing that no man could be perfect. I had become skilled at overlooking their shortcomings and normalizing the unhealthy behavior in my desperate pursuit of love. It was becoming clear to me that I had chosen emotionally unstable and unavailable men because my obsession with finding love had led me to romanticize their detrimental actions. Ultimately, I realized that my choice in partners was a reflection of the low level of self-love I had cultivated, stemming from my childhood wounds.

She then posed a question, asking what I had learned from my past relationships. While I knew there were valuable lessons I had gathered, articulating them all felt overwhelming. Sensing my hesitation, she gracefully stepped in, saying, "I'll tell you one thing, the relationships you had showed you what love is not."

Every word that flowed from the woman's mouth felt like a precious treasure, enriching me as our journey unfolded. Eventually, we reached an overlook surrounded by towering pine trees. She gestured toward the spot where we had stood a few hours earlier. She pointed out the first vortex we had visited, explaining that despite the canyons appearing far apart, they were all reachable within a single day. I was astonished by the apparent long distance, considering it had only been several hours since we stood there. It paralleled the feeling of fear distorting the perception of challenges, making them appear more daunting than they truly are.

The woman turned to face the north and drew my attention. "Look back here. That enormous rock is Heart Mountain," she said. To my surprise, I hadn't noticed it before, even though it hung above us, an immense heart-shaped rock in dark red hues.

"Stand tall, facing Heart Mountain, and close your eyes." Following her guidance, I stood upright, my gaze fixed on the mountain, and obediently closed my eyes.

"I want you to imagine your back full of daggers. These daggers have been stinging you for years. They hurt you, and you are in pain. Each dagger has a name. You decide what names you will give them based on what you have been carrying. It could be self-judgment, self-loathing, self-doubt, fear, et cetera. Now, I want you to focus on the dagger stuck in your back that is hurting you the most, the one that is causing a deep wound, the one that bleeds the most and has been hurting you the longest."

Following her instructions, I visualized my back invaded with daggers, representing the accumulated pain and wounds I had carried over the years, representing various burdens I had imposed upon myself. One dagger stood out among the rest, inflicting the deepest wound and causing the most prolonged suffering. It was the dagger of self-love—or rather, the lack thereof.

"How do I love myself?" I inquired.

"How do you show others you love them?"

"Hmm...I tell them I love them. I treat them kindly. I am empathetic to them. If I hurt their feelings, I apologize. I am patient with them. I give them compliments. When they hurt me, I forgive them. I try not to judge them and instead understand them."

The woman drew a striking parallel. "That is the exact same thing you must do for yourself," she exclaimed. "You must demonstrate to yourself how much you love you."

"But isn't self-confidence self-love?" I asked.

"Self-confidence is linked to the ego, but self-love is linked to your spirit."

Despite being seen as a strong, articulate, confident, and successful attorney to the outside world, I came face to face with the painful truth that I lacked self-love. The realization gripped me, and an overwhelming surge of emotions washed over me. It seemed astonishingly logical, yet it had eluded me for so long that I, too, deserved the same compassion, kindness, and empathy that I readily offered to others. I had neglected to extend forgiveness, patience, and understanding toward myself. It was a profound realization that I needed to prioritize my own well-being and cultivate a genuine love for myself. As I absorbed this revelation, I began to comprehend the path to self-love. Just as I express my love for others through words, acts of kindness, empathy, and forgiveness, I had to direct those same gestures inwardly. It was an eye-opening moment, and I felt a glimmer of hope that I could embark on a transformative journey toward self-love, gradually learning to see myself as an individual deserving of my own affection and care.

"I want you to slowly pull that dagger out from your back and feel its pain as you remove it. Bring it all the way out and hold it in your right hand." I visualized myself carefully pulling the dagger out from my back with a firm grip, feeling its sharpness pierce not only my physical form but also my emotional core. The weight of its impact began to unravel within me, stirring a mix of sadness, regret, and an undeniable longing for healing and self-acceptance. I pulled it completely out, feeling a profound release as its grip on me loosened. I held the dagger in my right hand, my trembling fingers enveloping its hilt. I cradled the dagger with both hands, as instructed. Shen then posed a question.

"What has this dagger taught you?"

The dagger symbolized the ways in which I had neglected myself and placed the needs and desires of others above my own. It taught me that while unconditional love for others is commendable, it should not come at the expense of my own self-love. I had been a pillar of support for Emilio's dreams, but I had failed to celebrate and pursue my own aspirations. The pursuit of an idealistic version of happiness had led to my own loss of identity. I had granted countless second chances to others, but had struggled to forgive and show compassion to myself. While I fought for justice for others, I had been unfair to myself, neglecting my own needs for fairness and self-care. I had diligently sought and admired the beauty in others, but failed to recognize and appreciate my own inherent beauty. I recognized the times when I had been my own worst enemy, harshly criticizing myself, doubting my capabilities, and taking responsibility for circumstances beyond my control. I had stifled my own instincts, hesitating to trust the innate wisdom within me. As these realizations flooded my consciousness, the pain intertwined with a newfound sense of clarity. It was time to release the self-imposed shackles, to offer myself forgiveness, kindness, and understanding. I needed to embrace my own dreams, nurture my well-being, and recognize my own worthiness of love and respect. With the dagger held before me, I made a silent vow to honor these lessons.

"You have transformed the negative energy that has held you back for so long. Going forward, instead of dwelling on the trauma or succumbing to self-doubt and self-judgment, you will draw upon these lessons held deep within your heart. They will be a source of strength and empowerment, guiding you away from negative self-talk and helping you make decisions that align with self-love. Stay committed to nurturing a positive and compassionate inner dialogue, treating yourself with the same kindness, respect, and understanding that you extend to others. These lessons will stand as beacons of self-empowerment, reminding you of your true value and encouraging you to embrace your authentic self.

I knelt on the dirt, my head bowed down and my palms touching the red, hot earth beneath me. Tears fell from my eyes, soaking the ground with each heavy drop. I allowed myself to surrender to the pain, to release the weight that had burdened me for far too long. The woman's gentle touch on my back reassured me that the suffering was coming to an end. The heavy cloak of self-doubt that had enveloped my being started to unravel. As I rose from the dirt, standing tall on my feet, I felt the solid ground beneath me. Facing the heart-shaped rock before me, I felt a surge of energy coursing through my veins. It was as if the mountain itself whispered words of encouragement, reminding me of my resilience and the incredible journey I had traversed. In that sacred space, with open arms, I embraced myself, acknowledging the incredible woman I had become. I celebrated my accomplishments, breaking free from the chains of societal expectations and carving my own path. I realized the profound impact of my choices on not only my own life but also on the lives of those who came before me and those who would follow. By pursuing higher education, I shattered the barriers of limited opportunities that had plagued my family for generations. By leaving an unhealthy and unhappy marriage, I became a beacon of hope for the women in my family, showing them that they, too, could reclaim their power and find happiness. Through my travels and explorations, I expanded my horizons, embracing a life filled with adventure and enriching experiences. In surrendering to the journey of healing, I broke the cycle of inherited pain, guilt, and self-loathing. Standing before Heart Mountain, I experienced a profound revelation: true love begins with self-love.

CHAPTER 20

Amor Eterno

I WAS SITTING ALONE BESIDE A TRANQUIL CREEK, SURROUNDED BY vibrant greenery and the abundance of nature. Perched on a rock, I wrapped my arms around my knees, marveling at the intelligence inherent in every living thing. Dragonflies danced in the air, their delicate wings glinting in the sunlight, as if they were celebrating my presence in this sacred place. It felt as though I was among dear friends. Observing the current of the water, I became captivated by its natural and effortless flow. Colorful leaves surrendered to the power of the current, allowing themselves to be carried along. In that moment, I yearned to be like those leaves—to surrender and be carried away by the flow of the universe. It seemed so much easier than trying to control and direct every aspect of my life.

Driven by this desire, I walked toward the middle of the creek and immersed myself in one of its deeper, larger pools. The crystal-clear water enveloped me, refreshing and reviving my spirit. Lying back, I allowed my body to float weightlessly, just like the leaves. The sound of the rushing water filled my ears, harmonizing with the rhythm of the creek. With my gaze fixed upon the vast expanse of white clouds and the boundless blue sky above, a familiar melody began to emerge. Soft notes of a violin gently accompanied the rustling of the trees surrounding the creek. Soon, the piano joined in, and the resounding chords of "Amor Eterno" became prominent. Euphoria washed over me as I recognized the tune—it was one that Mamá Juanita used to hum to me during my childhood, as she lovingly cradled me to sleep on her lap. The creek's waters enveloped me further, and I found myself completely immersed in the angelic moment. In an instant, I was transported to another place. Before me stood a long, wooden bridge leading to a sunflower field. Mamá Juanita, dressed in a flowing white tunic and leather huaraches, beckoned to me from the bridge's entrance. Overwhelmed with joy, I began to walk toward her, feeling the softness of the wood beneath my bare feet.

As I approached Mamá Juanita, my hand outstretched toward her, she gently grasped it, her touch tender and loving. However, in a soft whisper, she uttered words that pierced my heart, "Lucia, mi niña, you cannot come with me."

As I looked at Mamá Juanita, a deep sadness enveloped me. However, I adamantly followed her lead across the bridge. With each step, I felt as if I were floating, carried by an unseen energy that mirrored the way sunlight carried the notes of the melody through the air. Looking back, I saw Mamá Cuca, Doña Rosario and other women following, their angelic figures wrapped in white tunics. They smiled at me tenderly. Their presence filled me with warmth and encouragement as I made my way toward the sunflower field. One last glance at Mamá Juanita revealed a serene expression in her soft black eyes.

"Aún no es tu tiempo, Lucia," she whispered, the words flowing effortlessly from her lips. Suddenly, I felt the current of the creek wrap around my body, cradling me in a gentle embrace. Surrendering to its guidance, I trusted it to carry me downstream, alongside the colorful leaves.

My eyes opened. My mother stood by my side, her eyes wide with shock. "Lucia!" she exclaimed. "Mija, you're alive!" Overwhelmed with emotion, she threw herself onto my body, holding me tightly as tears streamed down her face. Confusion gripped me as I tried to grasp whether I was dead or alive. I clung to my mother, joining her in a heartfelt release of emotion. Then, a surge of emotions overwhelmed me as I realized that I had attempted and had failed to take my own life.

"Lucia, it's okay, Mija. I won't judge you. I know you've suffered so much." My mother spoke, her words cutting through the confusion and regret that swirled within me. She took my hand in hers and kissed it, her love and acceptance soothing my troubled soul. Seeing my mother by my side, remembering Mamá Juanita, a sense of solace washed over me. I wasn't sure why, but it was clear that God had a purpose for keeping me alive. Gradually, my desire to live and carry on began to rekindle.

***

A day after being released from the hospital, I lay in bed when my mother somberly entered the room. True to her nature as a Mexican mother, she simply opened the door without knocking, regardless of how old I had become.

"¿Mija, estás despierta?" she softly asked.

"Yes, Amá, come in," I replied, though she had already made her way into the room. "What's the matter, Amá?" Taking a seat by my feet, she looked at me with teary eyes. My heart clenched at the sight, and concern swelled within me.

"Amá, have you been crying? Amá, I'm sorry I caused you this pain and worry…" My words trailed off.

"It's not you, Lucia. Well, I am worried about you, but there's something else," she began, her voice laced with a mix of sadness and apprehension.

"¿Qué pasó, Amá? You're scaring me."

"It's Mamá Juanita. Ay, mija, I didn't want to say anything because I know you've had such a difficult time lately, and I didn't want anything else to torment you. But I know how much you love her." My heart sank, and worry etched its way across my face.

"Is she sick?" I asked, my voice filled with genuine concern.

"No, she is with God. She passed two days ago, while you were still unconscious," my mother revealed, her words hanging heavy in the air. A wave of disbelief washed over me, followed by a snowball effect of emotions. Was this somehow my fault? Had she known what I had done, and did it contribute to her passing? I needed to know.

"Amá, what happened to her? Did she know what I..." I couldn't finish my sentence, my voice faltering.

"She died peacefully in her sleep. She didn't know," my mother interjected gently, her eyes filled with both sadness and compassion. I was shocked, devastated by the news of Mamá Juanita's passing. But amidst the grief, a sense of relief washed over me. She hadn't known about my actions; she hadn't carried the burden of my struggle. Memories of my vision with her resurfaced in my mind. She had seemed so vibrant, so full of life as she guided me across the bridge. Jumping out of bed, urgency propelled me forward.

"Amá, we must go to her!" I said urgently.

"Hija, you're still recovering. I think it's best if Leticia or Pedro go with me. Your dad will stay behind to take care of you," my mother insisted.

"No, Amá, I must go too. *Necesito ir a verla.* I need to pay my respects in person," I persisted. Although my mother pleaded for me to stay behind and focus on my recovery, my longing to be close to my abuela was overpowering. It would be the last time I could see her, and the desire to be by her side overrode any rational concerns. I understood the weight of grief that my mother carried, as she mourned both my condition and the loss of Mamá Juanita. I felt guilty for putting her in such a difficult position, torn between caring for me in the hospital or being present for Mamá Juanita. I owed it to her to be strong and accompany her to see my grandmother one last time. A miracle had brought me back to life, granting my mother and me a chance to rush to my grandmother's side. I wasn't going to waste it. We embarked on a rushed trip back to El Romance to bid farewell to my beautiful abuela.

***

On the eve of my thirty-seventh birthday, I was back in El Romance. It was the day of Mamá Juanita's wake. I woke up five minutes before my alarm. Placing my right palm over my heart, I took a few deep breaths, acknowledging my second chance at life. I was there to honor and bury my beloved grandmother. Slowly, I rose from bed and sat on the edge, grounding myself as my bare feet touched the agave fiber rug beside me. Inhaling and exhaling, I allowed memories of Mamá Juanita's gentle embrace to wash over me. My heart was shattered, yet there was a profound connection that made me feel as if I had been with her all along in the last few days. I pressed a kiss to the picture of her on my phone and began to prepare myself for the day ahead.

The wake took place at Mamá Juanita's home in El Romance that afternoon. As we approached the house, I noticed a black bow hanging from the entrance, a somber symbol of mourning. It was also a reminder that she was gone. The door stood wide open, welcoming visitors to come and go. Stepping inside, the scent of flowers, burning candles, and copal filled the air, immediately embracing my senses. The patio was filled with people—relatives, friends, neighbors, and a mariachi band—some sitting in prayerful whispers, others shedding tears, and still others engaged in casual conversations, as if it were any other day. Children ran around, unaware of the weight of the moment.

Walking through the patio, we were greeted by cousins, aunts, uncles, nephews, nieces, and family friends, all rising to embrace us. My mother remained composed and collected, displaying her strength even in the face of devastation. I had always admired her unwavering demeanor. Though it was clear she was grieving, she remained strong for her siblings. Extended family members were present, including some I didn't recognize and cousins who had traveled from the States. It was impossible to greet everyone individually, so I made my way past the patio, eager to find the room where Mamá Juanita's body lay at rest. Following the fragrance of flowers and copal, I was guided toward the small cottage in the back of the house. The flickering candles inside confirmed that this was where she rested. Stepping into the room, I saw the wooden coffin adorned with an abundance of roses, marigolds, *cempasúchil*, and various other flowers. The sight was both beautiful and bittersweet. The coffin was open, and I began to make my way toward it when Aunt Matilde intercepted me.

"Lucia, mija, we think it would be wonderful if you could give a small speech in a few minutes. You have are the most eloquent among us, and considering your deep love for Mamá Juanita, it would be fitting for you to share a few words," Aunt Matilde suggested with a gentle smile.

"Of course, tía, it would be my honor," I replied, my voice filled with gratitude for the opportunity to pay tribute to my beloved grandmother.

"But before you do, there's something I need to give you," Aunt Matilde continued. From her bosom, she pulled out a folded piece of white paper and placed it in my hand, her eyes filled with a mixture of affection and anticipation.

"A few days before your Mamá Juanita passed, she called me into her room and asked me to help her write you a letter. She wanted you to get it before your birthday. She insisted that I write it and send it to you immediately. I got busy with things and unfortunately, a few days later she passed and with everything going on, I did not have a chance to send it. I'm sorry."

"It's okay tía, I can take it now."

I took the letter and felt compelled to read it immediately, even before seeing her resting in her coffin. A tear escaped me and

I proceeded to the corral, where Mamá Juanita kept her potted plants and chickens. I sat on a block of dried hay lying under the lemon tree and unfolded the letter.

Lucia:

For generations, the women of our family have been deprived of pursuing their dreams. Admitting that we had dreams would be a sign of rebellion, so we bowed our heads in submission. Our lives were defined in terms of being wives and mothers. We endured sacrifice, neglect and prohibition. I married your abuelo against my will. Then, I succumbed to the social pressure and pressed your mother to give up her dream of becoming a nurse so she could marry your father. The chains of patriarchy enslaved us for generations.

Since you were a little girl, I knew you were the light of our destiny. When you were born, you didn't cry like all newborns do; instead, you opened your eyes wide in amazement and smiled at me. You were always a curious child.

Although life has presented you with your own trials, you remained strong. You have dared to do things that others did not approve of. You followed your professional dreams despite the obstacles in your path. Along the way, you listened to the burning urge inside you to rebel against the norms of our family, our culture, and our religion. You broke the cycle of sad love stories that many women in our family have endured. While some have shamed you, don't blame them, Lucia. You should understand that for generations, we have seen ourselves as victims. We have failed to recognize that our sacrifices and struggles have made us strong survivors. We often boast about our physical strength, but only a few of us have had the courage to acknowledge the bleeding hearts beneath our thick skins. The experiences endured by me, your mother, and my mother provided examples of the life you should not accept. Lucia, you are brave. Your current circumstances do not define you. It is how you harness the challenges that will shape who you become. You have already set a different example for future generations. You must go on and become more than just a wife, or a lawyer. Become anything you desire to be, and in the process continue to be *brava*. I love you *mi niña*. Mamá Juanita.

As I finished reading the letter, the mariachi band began to play "Amor Eterno." Tears streamed down my face. The letter was a powerful testament to the strength and wisdom of my grandmother. She, too, had embraced bravery and spoken her truth in her final words to me. I was the ripple effect of her courage and sacrifice. Her letter renewed my zest for life. Overwhelmed with emotion, I ran to her coffin and came to a halt just before seeing her still body. As I approached slowly, her face came into view, radiating a serene peace. With deep respect, I bowed before her. She looked angelic in her white huipil. Her long, white hair was loose. Her black eyes, once full of life, were now peacefully closed. Leaning in, I pressed a gentle kiss to her forehead and whispered softly, "Thank you for taking care of me, abuela. Thank you for guiding me back to life. I promise I will continue to be *brava como tú* and seek to be the best and happiest version of myself."

The End

A NOTE FROM THE AUTHOR

Dear Reader,

First and foremost, thank you immensely for taking the time to read my first book. As a new author your support means so much. I truly hope you have enjoyed *Brava* and that you recommend it to anyone you think should read it.

In 2020, when pandemic hit, I began the process to bring this novel to life. As the city shut down, the streets became empty, and our lives were slowly disrupted, with nowhere to go, locked away at home in quarantine, and with extra time on my hands, I had no excuse but to finally write the book I always wanted to write. The pandemic came to shake us all up. For me, it was the beginning of an internal transformation that was very necessary. Everything that happened that year, intensified my fears and my insecurities and with nowhere to go, I had no choice but to sit with my feelings. Writing had always been my way of channeling my emotions, so I decided to give my repressed passion for creative writing a chance.

While this is a book born during a worldwide pandemic, the story had been slowly brewing in my mind throughout the years. Everything that transpired the years prior to the pandemic was preparing me to write *Brava*. Growing up as a first-generation Latina surrounded by other hard working and tenacious first-generation Latinx inspired this fiction novel. The first draft metamorphosed significantly because I wrote it with heightened emotions. I wrote from the wound. As I transformed and heladed, the manuscript did too. This book, its final version, was written by a healed and wiser version of me.

My hope is not merely to touch on various issues that first-generation Latinx face in their journeys to reach the so-called American dream. My hope is to go beyond. It is to take you back to the struggles of our ancestors and understand where we come from and how those struggles have paved the path for us. I pose the idea that obtaining an education and improving our socio-economic status, is not tantamount to true happiness as new challenges emerge and we must learn to navigate through them without a blueprint. My hope is to encourage you to think of the key moments in your own life where you were called to surrender, to see through the pain and the adversity that has occurred in your life and to use that as fuel to recharge and create the life you desperately yearn for. It is my hope that through Lucia's journey you appreciate your unique journey. While we are connected by a similar immigrant experience, your life has a uniqueness that adds richness to this world. Unlike what we have been told, life is about more than checking boxes and meeting social expectations. Our unique journeys hold the answer to our purpose and we must let them unfold like a flower.

My hope is that you understand that your survival has a deeper meaning than merely being resilient. I hope that this book provokes you to take time to examine your journey and ask yourself whether you are living the life you truly want. My hope is that after reading *Brava*, you ponder on your life and are courageous enough to make the changes that will unleash the passion that has been flickering in your heart for years, and not what society has been telling you, you should do. I hope *Brava* inspires you to live a life with no regrets, because if you have survived a worldwide pandemic, then you have been given a second chance. I hope that you gather everything life has thrown at you and use it to build a solid platform to create the life you are worthy of having. You can do this! You deserve to live a life that you love!

ACKNOWLEDGMENTS

This book is dedicated to my mother and my father, who have been and continue to be my biggest cheerleaders. I have never taken for granted the fact that they sacrificed their own dreams and lives to see mine flourish. Gracias Amá y Apá! Este libro es por y para ustedes.

It is also dedicated to my grandmothers and great grandmothers, who had no voice and endured physical, mental, and psychological abuse at the hands of a patriarchal society. My hope is that through this book, I can honor your power and your strength. May my healing make you proud and also liberate you *abuelas*. Thank you for paving the road for me to break unhealthy generational cycles.

It is dedicated to my sisters, Rosie and Fati, my brother, Fer, my nephew, Alex, and my cousin Vicente, with whom I spent most of the pandemic. Eating lunch with you on our patio, unable to go anywhere, having long, candid chats, and heart-to-heart conversations about our childhood created a beautiful bond between us that I deeply cherish. Your unwavering support through this process has been so essential. Thank you for sharing your life with me.

It is also dedicated to my coven of strong, intelligent, and badass hermanas/amigas: Sonia, Emir, Norma, Magdalena, and Elvira, thank you for never leaving my side and holding space for me vent through it all, the pretty and the ugly. Thank you for cheering me on this new path, jumping in to offer ideas, and read my manuscript.

It is also dedicated to all the first-generation Latinx lawyers who sacrificed so much to become advocates for our communities and continue to sacrifice their lives to help our gente while surviving in a profession that lacks adequate mentorship. Without your bilingual voice, your bicultural experiences, and your love and passion for a profession that is extremely sacrificial and overwhelming, many would be lost and helpless in a legal system that is far from being perfect.

It is dedicated to my coaches, therapists, family, and friends who held me lovingly through my healing process and lit a candle for me in this new journey as a writer. To my love, Michael, thank you for your support and encouragement during the times of self-doubt.

I want to thank and acknowledge two amazing Mexican authors who kindly donated their time to give me advice and guidance about writing my first novel: Maira Hernandez and Sandra Hinojosa Ludwig, mil gracias! Sandra, your advice and willingness to endorse my novel when no one else would, meant the world to me. Your kindness was a significant factor in encouraging me to keep going with this project and not lose faith. Maira, your optimism and your charisma made me believe in myself as a writer. I appreciate the ideas and feedback you have given me throughout the process.

I also want to thank my dear friend Dr. Emir Estrada and my editor, Silvestre Vallejo. I am forever grateful to you both for taking the time to read my manuscript and give me detailed advise during the tedious editing process. Your thoughts and guidance made an enormous difference.

This novel is dedicated to all immigrants who have had the courage to leave their beloved countries behind, risking it all, putting everything, including their lives, on the line, and starting from zero for the love of their families and for the desire to live dignified lives.

It is dedicated to all the first-generation Latinx, who have taken it upon themselves to stop vicious and toxic generational cycles that have harmed our people for decades. To those who have chosen to heal their trauma and had the courage to say, "It stops with me," I see you, I feel you, I am with you. You are not alone. *Por nosotros. Por nuestros ancestros. Por nuestro linaje.*

ABOUT THE AUTHOR

ADRIANA PALOMARES is a first-generation attorney, author, and entrepreneur. She is the product of resilience, ambition, and a deep connection to her Mexican roots. She was born in Guanajuato, Mexico. In the late eighties, her family migrated to the U.S., seeking a brighter future and escaping the looming shadows of poverty. She was raised in an impoverished neighborhood in Los Angeles dodging gangs, drugs, and low expectations.

Against all odds, she became the first member of her family to earn a college degree from UCLA and the only one to pursue a legal career, eventually graduating from law school and practicing at a renowned national law firm in Los Angeles. While her legal journey began by defending businesses and corporations, her heart led her toward a path of social justice. She found purpose in representing injured workers and providing legal assistance to communities of color in need.

Yet, amidst her legal pursuits, a passion for creative writing always burned within her. Her academic background in English, her love for literature, and her collection of poems and short stories lay the foundation for her future as a published author.

In her role as an entrepreneur, she has dedicated her time to promoting and preserving her Mexican culture and heritage through curated cultural experiences throughout Mexico. Additionally, she is an unwavering advocate for higher education within the Latinx and other underrepresented communities. She continues to share her experiences and insights as a mentor, conference panelist, and motivational speaker at educational conferences, striving to inspire others to reach for their dreams.

With *Brava*, her debut novel, she embarks on a new chapter

of her life as a published author. Adriana resides in Los Angeles, California, surrounded by her cherished family and friends. She is driven by a commitment to share stories that resonate with diverse audiences and a determination to celebrate the strength and richness of her Mexican-American identity.

Photo by Leroy Hamilton

Facebook.com/latinalegaltales/
Instagram:@latinalegaltales

Printed in the USA
CPSIA information can be obtained
at www.ICGtesting.com
LVHW040238011123
762645LV00001B/43